Dick Cady is a former journalist whose honours include the Pulitzer Prize, Associated Press Freedom of Information Award and George Polk Memorial award. He lives in Indianapolis.

THE EXECUTIONER'S MASK

Police Officer John Griffo died a hero in the line of duty. On national television, the entire country watched lifetime criminal J.J. Jackson shoot him in cold blood. But, facing death by lethal injection in seven days' time, Jackson insists that murder was never his intention. Attorney Sonny Ritter is trying to get his life back on track when his brilliant law school classmate Kit Lake asks him to work on J.J. Jackson's final appeal. To turn down this gorgeous blonde proves impossible and together they quickly uncover the seedy underworld of a corrupt city. Racing against the executioner's clock, Kit and Sonny must reveal the truth if Jackson is to go on breathing.

DICK CADY

THE
EXECUTIONER'S
MASK

Complete and Unabridged

ULVERSCROFT
Leicester

First published in Great Britain in 2005 by
Robert Hale Limited
London

First Large Print Edition
published 2005
by arrangement with
Robert Hale Limited
London

British Library CIP Data

Cady, Dick
    The executioner's mask.—Large print ed.—
Ulverscroft large print series: crime
1. Death row inmates—United States—Fiction
2. Lawyers—United States—Fiction
3. Suspense fiction 4. Large type books
I. Title
813.6 [F]

ISBN 1–84617–058–3

Published by
F. A. Thorpe (Publishing)
Anstey, Leicestershire
Set by Words & Graphics Ltd.
Anstey, Leicestershire
Printed and bound in Great Britain by
T. J. International Ltd., Padstow, Cornwall

This book is printed on acid-free paper

For Jo Ann

1

She was a frosted blonde up top and a natural blonde down below. She would have been naked except for the pink silk panties and the tattoo of a Venus's-flytrap on the inside of her left thigh, just below the panty line. A tiny arrow pointed in the right direction. The tattoo symbolized her name, Venus, she explained, not some interest in devouring her lovers.

When you're reduced to bringing home bar belles with botanical tattoos, you don't ask a lot of questions, because they're liable to tell you their life story as if it's an updated version of *Beowulf*. But this was one I couldn't resist.

'Do you know what a Venus's-flytrap is, honey?'

Venus refilled our glasses with Cutty and slipped back into bed. 'Sure, it's a man-eating plant.' Her voice had a sweet, squeaky quality.

'Uh, not really. An insect-eating plant.'

'Well,' she said with perfect seriousness, 'I guess it's the same thing,' an answer I had to admit had a certain metaphorical truth. 'Anyway, what about you? Is Sonny your real name?'

'Nickname. Short for Carson. Carson Talmadge Ritter III.'

'That's a lot of Ritters. So what do you do for a living?'

'I'm a lawyer. The son of a lawyer. The grandson of a lawyer.'

Venus offered a squeal of approval. 'Well, thank you for a man who isn't afraid to tell the truth. I thought about becoming a lawyer once. Because I saw this movie about a famous lawyer and putting monkeys on trial or something. The way some people treat animals is a crime.'

I sipped my drink. 'The monkey wasn't on trial, Venus. The theory of evolution was. The court decided we're all little gods with furry pubic hair to keep out the fleas.'

Venus twittered and rubbed her fingers along my bare chest.

'I like you, Sonny. You say funny things. I like going to bed with a lawyer. My lawyer wanted me to go to bed with him, you know, to knock down the fee, but I wouldn't. He was an old fatty. So, Mr Lawyer, how come you're living here instead of a mansion?'

Not knowing whether to laugh or cry, I pulled Venus on the pillow next to me. I had met her all of three hours ago in a neighborhood hangout called the Alley Cat Lounge. She beat me at three straight games of pool while replaying the same old Creedence song on the jukebox. She was delighted to learn I had an empty house and a full bottle less than a mile away. She didn't know the difference between Mozart and Mantovani but she decided Wolfie was a good accompanist for making love. She did so like someone rowing a boat, deliberately and rhythmically, with occasional grunts and squeals.

I was starting to like her. She had the gift of enjoying strangers. That counts for something, especially when you're nearing middle-age and accustomed to the conveyor-belt of disappointment and divorce. Her smile still had enough sincerity to radiate warmth over the wreckage on which I floated. She made me laugh. She made me forget. I knew we'd be friends until the Cutty ran out.

'I give all my money to orphans,' I said. 'Let's guess your real name. Delores? Amanda?'

'Heather. Heather Campbell. I've been married three times, so I've had four names. What kind of lawyer are you? I mean what kind of cases?'

'I chase ambulances, if you want to know the truth.'

'Really?' Her large baby-blue eyes lifted in surprise. 'Young, good-looking guy like you should be with one of them big fancy law firms downtown.'

'I'm an old thirty-five. Anyway, I've had a bit of a setback.'

'Do you want to talk about it?'

'It's a long, sad story, honey. A very sad story.'

'*Those* I've heard a lot of,' Venus said, her face momentarily forlorn. 'Told a few myself, too.'

'Did you come here to share biographies or to drink?'

She smiled and tickled the skin of my hip. 'I came here to party, if *you* want to know the truth. You're cute. The kind of cute I like.'

I climbed out of bed and wobbled to the dresser to get the bottle. Venus could hold her liquor, I'll give her that. She had consumed a generous portion of the Scotch since our first go-round, and she looked like she was lathering up for round two.

'You won't kick me out?' she said suddenly. 'I'll leave in the morning, okay? I'm not the type that likes to stick around. But I don't want to be calling a cab at midnight, either.'

'You've got a deal.'

The telephone rang.

Sitting on the nightstand under the window air conditioner, it rang five times before Venus said, 'Ain't you going to answer?'

'No.'

'Don't you have a recorder?'

'It's broken.'

The phone kept ringing.

'Guess they're not going to go away,' Venus predicted.

'You answer, then.'

She picked up the receiver.

'Hello? Yeah. Who? Yeah.' She looked at me with wide eyes. 'For you. The cops.'

I took the receiver. 'This is Sonny Ritter.'

'This is Captain O'Hara,' a sharp voice said. 'I run the police hostage team. Phillip Curry is barricaded inside his home and holding his two children hostage. He wants to talk to you.'

'Slow down a minute, captain. Phil's an ex-client, not a client. Repeat what you just told me.'

'We don't have time, Ritter. You want to risk the lives of two little kids? Now, I have your address in Broad Ripple. I'll have a squad car there in a few minutes. You be ready. Curry has a rifle and two pistols, and he's talking pretty crazy.'

The dial tone returned.

'Trouble?' Venus asked.

'Yeah,' I said, reaching for my underwear. 'I think one of my clients wants to pay me for my services.'

2

The black-and-white raced through the night at sixty miles an hour, with red and blue lights flashing and siren screaming. I sat rigidly in the front seat, wanting the ride to end and dreading what might happen when it did. I knew Phil Curry had been hanging on the edge. I also knew what he was capable of.

The stone-faced driver decelerated as we reached the neighborhood. It was your average all-American, middle-class residential area with ranch homes, mature trees, and a Neighborhood Crime Watch no one used much. Now it had been transformed into an eerie moonscape surrounded by barricades, police cars, and clusters of curious neighbors. I had seen something like this before, in the night desert of Iraq. I remembered a strange slow-motion world where the nearness of death dried your throat, tightened your scrotum, and made your heart pound.

We moved past a sawhorse and through a line of cops wearing helmets and flak jackets and holding rifles with scopes. Ahead, Curry's white-and-brick home stood out like a tourist site. Huge spotlights blanketed it with a kind of ghostly daylight and made everything around look darker. A police helicopter focused two more funnels of light on the roof. A half-dozen squad cars were lined up along the street, two of them blocking the asphalt driveway. Snipers were positioned behind them. I could see dark figures crouched behind the lilac bushes.

The driver turned off the lights and stopped behind a large iron-gray van that resembled an armored car.

'Captain's inside,' he said.

I felt a chill when I stepped outside. I trembled even though it was July and still near eighty and fireflies could choke on the humidity. Blame the drinking. Blame the image of Curry sitting inside that house debating whether to kill Danny and Melissa before he sucked on his .38. I didn't want any part of Phil's nightmare. But apparently he wanted me.

'Here's the lawyer,' someone announced when I stepped inside the van.

It was roomier than it looked from outside, and filled with an array of electronic equipment. There were closed-circuit television pictures showing all four sides of the house, two computer screens flashing data in green lines, and a third screen showing what appeared to be infrared images from inside the house. Two officers in blue uniforms glanced at me with bright eyes and turned back to their work.

O'Hara was a beefy man wearing the white uniform shirt of command. Somewhere between fifty and sixty, he had a chunky face, as Slavic as it was Irish; flared eyebrows, thin lips, sea-gray eyes, and a throaty voice that sounded like it had been rubbed over a colander.

He motioned me to a chair and didn't offer to shake my hand.

'Ex-client, you say. How long ago?'

'Three years. I haven't seen Phil in more than a year. I was out of commission for two years.'

'Yeah, we know,' O'Hara said, unable to suppress a note of contempt. 'What I want to know now is everything you can tell me about Curry.'

I rubbed my forehead and decided Phil had waived any privilege, not that I knew a lot of his secrets. Except one. I knew he was paranoid.

'He was a special agent for the FBI. Brick agent. He had a good record. He didn't like some of the things that were going on in the office, so he became a whistle-blower. The bureau sent in a squad from OPR — that's the Office of Professional Responsibility

— and they whitewashed everything. Everybody made Phil's life miserable. He resigned, hired me, and we filed a federal lawsuit. It was thrown out about a year later. He was, is, very bitter. Then his wife left him. When I used to talk to him, he brooded a lot and wrote letters to the editor.'

'Blew the whistle about what?'

'Political corruption. Police corruption. Agents were cataloging information about payoffs and not opening cases.'

For five or six seconds O'Hara stared at me with a look that made me think of an approaching iceberg. Then he said, 'How would you describe his mental condition?'

I didn't know how candid I could be. Or whether my nonmedical opinion ought to sway whatever decisions O'Hara had to make.

'A lot of strain,' I said. 'Anger, of course. The feeling of being abandoned. Of getting shit on for trying to do the right thing. The feeling that everybody's against him. In the beginning, he had supporters. But they bailed out because the thing is such an obsession with Phil.'

O'Hara grunted. 'I know the type. Do-gooders who think the world's against them. How were you getting along last time you talked to him?'

'Reasonably okay, I'd say. Phil held out

hope I could turn things around. I tried to deal with him realistically. He wants to push, push, push. I like the man, but he's caught in the whistle-blower's syndrome.'

'Which is what?'

'It's hard to explain. If you're in any kind of big organization or bureaucracy, you have to be a little crazy to buck the system. I don't mean literally crazy, but, you know, willing to risk everything. And when the organization comes back and slams you to the canvas, and you end up losing everything, well . . . '

O'Hara waited for me to continue. Instead I hit him with a question.

'What set him off now, if you know?'

'He got fired this afternoon. Security guard job. He's been living in a rented room. Around five o'clock he shows up here, yells at the neighbors, and walks in with some weapons. We know the kids are inside. We're not sure about his wife.'

'Linda, his ex-wife.'

'Anyway, he's willing to talk. He wants to talk. He wants to talk to you.'

'I'll be glad to do what I can. I assume you're taping all phone conversations.'

A half-moon smile broke across the captain's face.

'No, no, not on the phone. He wants to talk to you face to face. You're the only one he'll

10

let inside. We're willing to give it a chance, but we can't wait forever. Curry says he'll take one more call. The call saying you're on your way in.'

The chill returned, followed by a queasy sensation. I wished I hadn't spent most of the evening drinking. For some odd reason, I wondered if Venus's cab had picked her up. I thought about different things in order to avoid thinking about walking into that house with a dozen or more police guns trained on me and a desperate ex-fed waiting inside with an arsenal.

O'Hara probably could read my thoughts. He cleared his throat.

'Look, Ritter, my reading is he's probably close to the edge, but not over. He knows exactly what's going on out here. Now, we have a good track record. We bring 'em back alive. But any time a man is under a lot of stress and has weapons at hand, no one can predict what might set him off. What I'm saying is, you don't have to go in. On the other hand, there's the kids. The boy's twelve, the girl's ten. You might be able to talk some sense into the man.'

'I'll go in.'

'Good. Now let me tell you what you're not going to do. No sudden moves. No hero bullshit. No arguing with him. You agree,

agree, agree. You tell him this is all misdemeanor stuff so far, and it doesn't have to go farther. Hell, tell him you'll represent him. If you can get him to come out, fine. If not, well, you get out. Understand?'

'Yes.'

'Now, do this. Look at everything you can look at. When you come out, I'll want you to tell me exactly what the layout is, everything you can think of. And when you come out, come out with your hands on top of your head. Do everything slowly, very slowly.'

'Yeah, well, I'm not breathing slowly.'

The half-moon smile came back.

'We know about your troubles. You work things out here, maybe you can score some points for yourself.'

'You don't know a damned thing about me,' I said. 'I'm a lawyer in good standing. I don't need your innuendo.'

'Okay, okay. You just follow instructions and we'll see if we can end this thing. Take off your jacket and belt.' He turned to look at an officer at one of the consoles. 'Right. Patch me in to Curry.'

O'Hara picked up a black telephone from which a halfdozen wires protruded.

'Mr Curry, this is Captain O'Hara. Look, Mr Ritter's here and he wants to come in. You still agreeable? Good, good. Now, I see a way

12

out here. Listen to your lawyer. Everything's going to be fine. We can end this in a satisfactory way for everyone. That's what we all want, isn't it? Good. He'll be on the porch in a minute.'

We stepped into the night air. For some reason I suddenly felt resolute. I would need all my wits. The thing not to do was say anything Phil would see right through.

Be calm, reasonable, and think.

'Remember,' O'Hara said, 'no sudden moves. Walk slowly, carefully. Make this thing happen, okay?'

'Okay.' It came out in the whispery tone of an edgy man walking into a tunnel in danger of collapsing.

3

The steps were concrete, the porch wooden. There was an old-fashioned glider hanging by chains. A wicker basket of fake wildflowers sat by the door. A white aluminum kid's scooter lay on its side. The screen door was closed and the front door behind it open. My shoes made a clunking sound.

I tapped on the door.

'Phil, it's me. I'm coming in.'

'Yeah, come in, Sonny,' Phil called in a hollow voice.

I opened the screen door and closed it gently behind me. All the lights were on in the living room, and everything appeared to be exactly where it should be, as if the room had just been cleaned and vacuumed. The furniture was a mixture of modern and Early American, and the sofa and chairs had lacy white doilies on the arms. A painting of a sailboat leaving a harbor covered the largest wall. A stack of magazines with *Time* on the top sat next to the easy chair. The room smelled of furniture polish and cat litter.

The light from the kitchen spilled on to the living room carpet. I walked to the entryway.

'You don't have a gun or anything, do you?' Phil said.

'Absolutely not. They even made me take off my belt. I wish the hell I had something to drink, though.'

'Well, come on in.'

If you want to see a sight to scare the living hell out of you, walk into a modern kitchen where sitting at the table is a sad-faced man who's been crying, and his hand is resting on a shiny black revolver with a long barrel, with another revolver and a rifle within reach, and you can't shake from your mind the idea that behind his forced and forlorn smile is the melancholy resolve to kill you and every living thing around.

Curry, I calculated, would have just turned forty. He was about five-eight, with a muscular frame, large hands, and receding brown hair, gray at the sideburns. He had gentle brown eyes and a hawk nose. I couldn't see his pants, but his shirt was part of a brown uniform that had two-inch gold patches on the shoulders.

He cleared his throat. 'I gotta tell you, Sonny, it'd be a real mistake to try anything.'

I sat across from him at the table.

'Look, Phil. I didn't ask for this. You did. You wanted me. So I'm glad to help. Let me mediate this thing. Remember, I'm your

15

lawyer. The last thing I'm going to do is pull some stupid stunt.' I tried to lighten my voice. 'You know me. I'm a lover, not a fighter.'

It didn't come out sounding like I thought it would. It sounded like I wouldn't fight for him.

'Yeah.' Phil said in a mournful voice. I noticed most of his fingernails had been gnawed to the flesh. 'You told me we could win the damn thing. I thought we could. In the end, they ran over me with a steam-roller. I lost everything. My job, my wife, my home, my kids. My self-esteem.'

'But you did the right thing,' I said evenly. 'You can always hold your head high. You were right and the bureau was wrong. But you know the motto. Don't embarrass the bureau. Hell, you told me that.'

He smiled a smile of bitter acknowledgement. A coffee cup that said GOLFERS ONLY sat near his left hand. His right hand rested on the butt of the black revolver.

'Yeah, well,' he said, 'that was then and this is now. I'm not mad at you, Sonny. I know you stuck your neck out. You gave it your best shot. Heck, I know you discounted some of your fees. I didn't call you here to do an autopsy on the past.'

'Then why did you ask for me? Half the

damned police department is outside. There's no reason for any further commotion. Mostly, I think, they're worried about the kids.'

Phil nodded in such a way that it looked like he was bowing his head in shame. His eyes had a glazed look. The sink faucet was dripping. On the shelf above, a peach-colored placard said GOD BLESS THIS KITCHEN. The linoleum counter held a ceramic figure of a spit-curled boy with the words MOM I LOVE YOU.

'Them and me both,' Phil said, taking a deep breath. 'That's what I want to talk to you about. Listen, why don't you check on them? They're in the bedroom. They're scared, and I don't know how to reassure them.'

'You're sure you want me to check on the kids?'

'It's okay. Really.'

As slowly as I could I stood up from the chair and walked towards the bedrooms. I remembered the general layout from better times. There was a hallway off the kitchen going past the bathroom and splitting in two directions, left for the master bedroom and right for the smaller one. There were no lights on, but the light from the kitchen provided enough illumination. I could hear the faint *thump-thump* of the helicopter high above the house.

The carpet in the hallway was gray and frayed. An old-fashioned walnut stand stood against one wall holding a purple ceramic bowl filled with silk flowers. On one beige wall was an arrangement of family pictures with old black-and-white photos on top and color studio portraits below, including the four Currys in happier times. As I turned towards the children's room, I glanced in the direction of the master bedroom. The door was open and Linda's bare legs had splayed a few feet into the hallway, the bare feet pointing in opposite directions.

I froze for a second. She lay on her back and her eyes were open but not seeing anything. Part of her forehead was gone, with a kind of jelly of blood and brains in its place. Her right hand was open and the fingers were spread, as if she had been trying to catch a ball when she fell backwards. She had on a lavender short-sleeved blouse and white walking shorts showing several red ink-blot patterns. The red paint of her toenails resembled the random blotches of blood on her skin.

I fought back nausea and turned to the other room. I had been sweating all along, and now I felt like I was drowning in sweat.

It was dark, but so much light flowed through the shades it might have been daylight. When I saw the two shapes in the bed I thought they were dead. When I stood

18

over them I saw them trembling.

'Hello, kids,' I said in a gentle, raspy voice. 'Do you remember me? I'm Mr Ritter. I'm an attorney. You can call me Sonny. Are you okay?'

Danny and Melissa lay on their backs with a sheet pulled up to their chins. They were absolutely rigid except for the trembling. Their faces were stark white and glistening with sweat, petrified in terror. The girl had black hair cut in a page boy; her brother sandy hair cut in a flattop.

I touched each on the face and kept my voice as soft as I could.

'Listen, kids, I'm here to help, okay? Everything's going to be just fine. Your dad's going to be fine. You just stay here a few more minutes and, please, don't move.'

Neither said anything. Their eyes bulged at me. I was afraid if I tried to touch them again they would leap into my arms. I didn't want to disturb anything. They had to know their mother lay ten or twelve feet away with part of her face missing.

Suddenly Melissa's hand grabbed mine. She moved so quickly I jumped. Her little fingers clamped on my wrist with the power of someone clutching the side of a cliff. There was no way I would ever be able to describe the sheer terror I saw in her eyes.

As carefully as I could, I forced a smile and released her hand.

'I'll be back in a few minutes,' I whispered.

I backed out of the room.

My skin felt creepy and my mouth was dry. In the kitchen, Phil hadn't moved, and the hand near the gun hadn't moved. His face was sweaty and pasty white. Now I could see dark underarm stains on his shirt. I wondered if he knew what planet we were on.

'Yeah, they're okay,' I said in a voice as calm as I could muster. 'They're scared. You need to end this thing, Phil.'

'You're right about that,' Phil said in a froggy voice. 'Listen, Sonny, you remember my sister, don't you? If something happens to me, she wants the kids. I'm worried about the goddamned government. The government might try to take them. The welfare department, the bureaucrats, the ball-busters.'

'I'll do anything I can to help.'

'You're a good guy,' he said. 'You won't let the state take the kids, will you? You'll help my sister if she needs help.'

'You have my word. My word of honor.'

Phil nodded, as if my pledge had been unexpected, and he was grateful.

'Then like you say, let's end this.'

'That's the right thing to do.'

'You go out. Take all the guns. Tell them

I'm coming out. Then everybody can go home. And my sister gets the kids.'

'I guarantee she will. Did you say you want me to take the guns?'

'Absolutely. And I want to thank you, Sonny. Just having you here makes me feel better.'

'You're sure you want me to take the guns?'

Phil patted my hand. The touch of his flesh made me recoil. My stomach was churning. My mouth was so dry my tongue felt as big as a tennis shoe.

'I'm sure. Let's get this over with. I know the drill. Tell O'Hara I'll come out on the porch, put my hands on my head, and kneel down. No bullshit. Just end it.'

'That's the ticket. That's the thing to do. Just remember one thing, will you? Don't say anything. Not a word. Once you're in custody, let me do the talking for you.'

'Right. You can click on the meter right now. It'll be like old times.'

He handed me the revolver, then the second revolver, then the rifle, all with a smile of resignation.

I was so relieved I wanted to shout with joy. Instead I kept my cool. The thought of walking out on that porch with three weapons gave me pause.

'Okay,' I said. 'I'll tell O'Hara.'

'Right. Be careful, Sonny. They're all loaded.'

Phil grinned. For a second, I saw the brave, intelligent face from the past.

'Guns make me nervous,' I said. 'See you in a few minutes.'

I had a creepy feeling along my back, but nothing happened. I stopped at the screen door.

'This is Ritter,' I yelled. 'I'm coming out. I have the weapons. Do you understand? This is Ritter.'

'Come on out,' a voice said over a bullhorn.

Entering the house, I had the lights behind me. Leaving, I walked into them, a blinding wave of whiteness. I was shaking so badly I thought I might drop the rifle. I came down the steps and walked as slowly as possible towards the street. Every little sound might have been a rifle being cocked.

I heard O'Hara's voice.

'Give them to this officer, and step back.'

'He's coming out,' I announced. 'He's not armed.'

'Step back out of the way,' O'Hara said.

I moved back three or four steps and turned, standing in the perimeter of light about thirty feet from the porch.

To my surprise, Phil's voice boomed out.

'I'm coming out!'

'Step out with your hands on your head and drop to your knees,' O'Hara commanded over the bullhorn.

The door opened. Phil stepped into the light, a spectral figure frozen momentarily in the overwhelming glare. He took two steps and stood there with his hands behind his head.

'Drop to your knees,' O'Hara ordered.

'He's got a gun!' someone yelled.

It happened in a blurry moment that somehow slowed down in a strange, compressed bubble of time. Phil's right hand moved away from his head, waving a small dark object. In a microsecond there was an explosion of sounds, a synchronized chorus of gunfire like a firing squad responding to a signal.

The SWAT men were deadly accurate. The impact of a series of direct hits threw his body backwards against the porch wall. He crumpled downward with holes the size of olives from his stomach to his head. The only change in the porch wall behind him was the sudden appearance of tomato-sized blotches of blood and tissue.

The firing stopped as quickly as it started but it seemed as if the reverberations of sound had been halted and held by the hand of time, and hung in my ears for minutes.

When I looked, men in helmets were on the porch, prodding Phil with their weapons. But he didn't move and never would move again.

Cops were running in every direction now. Two SWAT members led two policewomen inside. I stood there as if I had just fallen off the top of a building. I was stunned, dizzy, and disoriented.

The next thing I heard was O'Hara's voice.

'You did everything you could, Ritter. It's not your fault. I was afraid he might be an SBC.'

'What? A what?'

'A suicide by cop. I was hoping against hope.'

'I don't know what you mean.'

'Some people who want to kill themselves can't pull the trigger. So they try to force us to do it for them. We're trained to watch for this, but we can't take chances. Curry had a little .22 tucked in the back of his collar. A little .22, maybe shoot the wing off a bee. What the hell, how are we supposed to know?'

'Jesus,' I said.

'Yeah, it's not a pretty sight. Go ahead and puke your guts. Then I'll have an officer take you home.'

4

People who don't know anything about America's heartland used to think of Indianapolis as a kind of bus stop between Chicago and Cincinnati where most of the men look like Hoagy Carmichael and sit around chewing bits of straw under Royal Crown Cola signs. Progress changed the image, if not the reality.

Progress transformed Indianapolis into Indy, a city of gleaming buildings, pro sports teams, efficient interstate highways, and unified government. Progress chased away the hicks and brought in the slicks, who began promoting the town as a kind of Chicago without the sprawl. The new image was simultaneously true and false. Indy was a modern city and a good place to live and work, if you had the money. If you didn't, and especially if you didn't have Palmolive white skin, Indy had slums as ugly as any in Detroit or St Louis, and other lower-class neighborhoods where the residents had the same standing lepers had in the middle ages. Progress also brought heavy traffic, polluted air, a crowded airport, and the other amenities of being a modern city. To be honest, I had had just about as much progress as I could stomach.

The downtown did gleam at times. The tallest building was so tall it had a light tower to signal airplanes. It was called the American United Life building, and two complete floors were occupied by the law firm of Ritter Ritter Talmadge & Stokely. The first Ritter was my late grandfather, the two-term U.S. senator and one of the co-founders. The second Ritter was my father, the former congressman, unsuccessful Republican candidate for mayor, and member of all the country clubs that had at least one token black member, or, as my father used to say, colored member.

There would be no third Ritter ampersanded to this hallowed firm. The kind of law I pursued was not the kind of law my father cherished, because it didn't involve corporations, institutional pecksniffery, and obscenely large fees. My kind of law centered on little people caught on the criminal justice treadmill or stuck under the boot of indifferent bureaucracy. If ever there had been the slightest chance of a third Ritter, well, when the son who bears your name and shares your profession is busted for possession of cocaine and suspended from practice for two years, the door is sealed with rivets.

26

Carson Talmadge Ritter, Jr, and I seldom communicated. We saw each other on rare, unavoidable occasions, usually holidays where the family sat around like patients in an internist's office wondering who has the largest hemorrhoids. Nor did I visit the venerable offices in hopes the partners might send an evicted widow my way. But I followed an unusual ritual. Every morning I telephoned the firm before it opened.

I would call a certain number and a recording would answer, and a voice would say, 'Hi, this is Meg Thomas. I can't take your call right now, but if you'll leave your name and number I'll call you as soon as possible. Thanks, and have a nice day.' I would listen to her voice and whisper something silly, something like, 'I love you,' and hang up before the recorder kicked in.

Meg was a legal secretary in my father's firm, and his former daughter-in-law. I communicated with her even less than I did with him. The marriage had started unraveling before my troubles, and after my troubles her last words to me were, 'Sonny, how could you?' What she meant was, 'Sonny, how could you be so stupid?' Ever since then she hung up whenever she heard my voice. So I phoned her number each morning to hear her recorded voice, to feel the twinge in my heart, and to wonder how I could have been so stupid to let such a wonderful woman slip out of my life.

Usually I called in the early dawn from the bedroom of the house Meg and I once shared in Broad Ripple. It's a modest frame cottage home perfectly suited for the area, which is a kind of local version of Georgetown. Situated near a scenic canal and a winding river, Broad Ripple is filled with quaint shops, excellent restaurants, art galleries, used bookstores, and other casual spots that lure in shoppers and tourists.

From the house I could walk to the small office I had on the boulevard just below the canal. I had a renovated former barbershop next door to a dentist's office. I spent a lot of time staring out the window wondering how many wrong moves you can make in one lifetime and serving a handful of clients who didn't know or care their lawyer had bitten into a D-felony for drugs.

At the moment, I was staring at the front-page newspaper story chronicling the death of Phil Curry. In a one-column color photograph, Captain Milton O'Hara looked grimly disappointed. I had just told a TV reporter I didn't want to be interviewed, and slammed down the phone.

I was thinking, too. I was thinking Captain

Milton O'Hara had known more than he wanted to tell me.

Once the shock of watching a troubled former client die in a hail of bullets started wearing off, the events of the evening rolled through my mind with more clarity. O'Hara, for instance, almost certainly knew Phil had shot poor Linda. The gun would have made a noise, and the neighbors would have told the police. Then there was the infrared screen. Although I didn't pay much attention at the time, I now realized O'Hara and his people knew exactly how many human bodies, warm or not, were inside that house.

So O'Hara knew Curry had murdered his wife and might kill his children and his lawyer before he killed himself. O'Hara had elected not to tell me any of this. And if he had, what then? If I had known there was a murdered woman inside, would I have gone in anyway? I didn't know, and maybe that's why O'Hara didn't tell me everything.

The only thing I knew for certain was that Phil had committed suicide, just as if he had pulled the trigger himself. And it would be a long time before the shock completely went away. The evening was like a nightmare movie that kept playing and replaying on a screen inside my brain.

I did have one appointment. A neighborhood lady who wanted advice about cutting her green-haired granddaughter out of her will was scheduled to drop by. When the door opened I expected to see a gnarled hand clutching a cane. Instead I saw something unexpected. I saw Beauty with a capital B, as in Katherine Lake.

'Hi, Sonny,' Kit said. 'I hope you're okay.'

My voice lifted as it always did since the first time we met in law school. 'Kit. Sorry. Come in. My mind was a thousand miles away.'

'I can understand why,' she said, showing those terrific legs as she sat in the chair across from my desk. 'You must be a wreck.'

Some women are endowed with beauty, some with intelligence. Kit was one of those lucky creatures blessed with an abundance of both. And she had something not all beautiful women have, a quality called class. She was the whole gift-wrapped package, a super lawyer, a former deputy prosecutor, and a full partner in my father's law firm. She was also a friend of my ex-wife. And my friend. The only thing she wasn't was my lover. Which didn't mean I had to stop trying.

A natural strawberry blonde, Kit was tall, slender, and leggy, and blessed with the kind of complexion little girls have and older women covet. There wasn't a law firm in six states that didn't want to hire her, and not just because men on juries wouldn't be able to take their eyes off her. She had graduated first in our class and only gotten better since.

Let me tell you a crazy thing. Comparing Kit to Meg, Kit was prettier, sexier, and smarter. Men would crash Rolls-Royces into utility poles just to get Kit to turn her head, and not look a second time at Meg. Millionaires would burn their bankbooks for Kit and fling nickels at Meg. But I liked Kit and I loved Meg, and I think that's one of the reasons why Kit liked me. Don't ask for further explanation. Meg had burrowed into my heart and set up permanent residence, and there's not a library of books that can explain why. Love, obviously, is a state of confusion. Divorce is just a state of emergency.

Kit wore a shapely white linen suit set off with a ruby red scarf, matching heels, and a shiny red purse about the size of a duffel bag. From the sides of her strawberry blonde hair ring-shaped golden earrings shone. She brushed around the chair with a handkerchief because the cleaning service hadn't been around in weeks.

'You think you know how you'd react to these things, and you don't,' I said. 'I'll tell you this. When I got home I cried my eyes out.'

'Does it help to talk?'

'I don't know. I don't know much about anything. You should have seen those kids. The sight of those kids . . . '

'You did everything you could for Curry, didn't you?'

'Yeah, of that I'm confident. You know, when the whole thing came up originally, I really thought we were going to kick the federal government right in its fat ass. It was the good guys against the bad guys. Phil did the right thing. It took guts to do what he did. And do you know what the FBI did? They painted a big R on his back, R for rat. And after they shut him up, they transferred every damned agent he'd complained about. In other words, they did what they should have done in the first place. Only they weren't going to give Phil Curry any credit, because Phil Curry committed a mortal sin. He blew the whistle.'

When Kit frowned, as she did now, it showed freckles around her dimples. Kit made you notice things about her.

'I'm sorry,' she said. 'Sorry you had to see him die like that.'

'Well, I'll get over it. You know the Ritters. Old blood, stiff upper lip, what? Can't worry just because a client gets mowed down by the police, what?'

Kit smiled. 'At least you retain a little bit of your sense of humor.'

'It's the only thing that sustains me, Kit. I eat humor for breakfast and lunch. I skip dinners. Clients, you'll notice, aren't exactly beating down the door. It'll take time.'

'You'll be surprised how quickly people forget,' she said to encourage me.

I ran my hand through my sandy hair and shook my head at the injustice of justice.

'You want to know the ironic thing? To this day I've never tasted, smoked, snorted, or sniffed cocaine. One stupid decision ruins my life, and I don't even get to find out what the fuss is all about.'

'You were upset because of what was happening with Meg. It clouded your judgment.'

'You can say that again. Smart boy, me. So smart I decide to try cocaine one time. So smart I let one of my stupid unreliable clients set me up. I'm lucky they didn't throw the book at me.' I rocked back and forth to calm down. 'Sorry. You know all that. You're one of the few of my brother lawyers who stood by me.'

Kit made a face. '*Brother* lawyers? Sonny, please.'

'Okay, one of my few legal siblings. I feel better already, Kit. I feel better just being with you. You remind me of my measure as a man. You make me think of manly things, like getting you naked and anointing your body in some ancient biblical ritual. Just you and me in a luxurious suite at a Motel 6. Sound good?'

'Sonny, you're hopeless. I know you still have a thing for Meg.'

'Well, maybe I do. I'm just offering you a mad, meaningless sexual fling, that's all. Free, too.'

Kit suppressed a laugh. 'Thank you, and no. And I've come with an offer for you. I need help. Seriously. I'm handling the final appeal for J.J. Jackson.'

It was my turn to laugh.

'Right. The state of Indiana is going to give Jackson the big needle in what, a week or so? His case has been beaten to death, pardon the use of the word. Half the world saw him murder a cop, and you want to save him at the last minute? Katherine, please. I'm not in a mood for gallows humor.'

Her expression changed to that serious look she usually put on when she was about to explain something to someone who didn't want to hear her explanation.

'I'm serious, Sonny. Will you hear me out?'

'I'm all ears. Well, ninety-percent ears, anyway.'

Kit stood in front of the window, looking at a half-dozen geese and ducks waddling towards the canal.

'No jokes, please,' she said in a sober tone. 'Look, all the usual last-minute appeals are going forward by all the usual anti-death penalty lobbies. Jackson's mother wants something more, needs something more. She scraped together some money in order to hire, I don't know, a top legal talent to make sure everything possible is being done that can be done. I know it's late, but that's not the worst. I'm up to my ears in the legal niceties, trying to create anything to convince the Supreme Court or the parole board to at least delay the execution. I'm just over-booked. I don't have time to do any of the legwork on the factual stuff.'

'And you want me to do it?'

'Yeah, actually.'

'You must think I'm the patron saint of lost causes.'

Kit looked demure. 'Yeah, actually.'

I stood up and paced around the office. As much as I admired Kit, I wondered if she had allowed her heart to get in the way of her judgment.

'Look, Kit, the chances of finding any new

legal issue or overlooked exculpatory fact are virtually nil, you know that. Skip the virtually. This is a waste of the woman's money.'

'I told her.'

'Her son killed a cop on television, for crying out loud. He all but confessed. Hell, he did confess. What else? Oh, yeah, he's a sort of despicable career criminal, not some misguided ghetto angel who writes books or started a prison ministry. No one gives a shit about Jeremiah Jackson.'

'His mother does.'

I sat back down. 'Another thing. This cop, this Johnny Griffo, he was a *hero*. He's practically been canonized. You go to bat for Jackson, you insult everybody who hallows Griffo's memory.'

'Yes, you will.'

I raised my hand. 'Wait a minute. Does my father have anything to do with this?'

'Nope. Oh, he knows I'm making an offer, but it's my call. I'm sure if he had a voice, he'd disapprove. Of course I thought that would provide you with incentive.'

'Ms Lake, let me be honest. I'm not interested. I'd feel guilty because it would be cruel to raise his mother's hopes one iota. You know I'm against the death penalty, and if there's anything along legal lines I can do, I'll be glad to help. But to dig into the old case, eight years old, well . . . '

'You're a good lawyer, Sonny. One reason you're a good lawyer is you're a good digger. Into facts, not law books. That's how you supported yourself for two years, doing legwork, isn't it?'

'Yeah, when I wasn't sitting on dull surveillances for private investigators who used to work for me. Or delivering pizzas. I'd like to help you, Kit, but . . . '

'No way I can change your mind?'

'Well,' I said wolfishly, 'are you saying certain things are negotiable after all?'

'No. I'm saying that if you say yes, I'll write you my personal check for five thousand dollars, right here and now. What's your answer?'

'My answer is yes. Forget everything I said before that.'

'I knew you couldn't say no to a hopeless cause. In fact, I'm having the transcripts sent over. They'll be arriving any minute.'

Kit smiled cleverly as she took out her checkbook.

'Oh, one other thing. We're having breakfast tomorrow with the governor's chief of staff. At the Skyline Club. You'll have to wear a tie.'

5

Actually, to use one of Kit's favorite words, Jeremiah Jackson didn't kill Sergeant Griffo on television. Close, but not exactly.

Griffo was leading a squad of officers serving warrants. They tracked down Jackson and a companion in crime to a house in a lower middle-class section on the east side of town. A unit from the British Broadcasting Company was in the city filming a segment for a prototype of a BBC program modeled on *COPS*. The Brits were videotaping Griffo's team, and the camera looked on as the six officers surrounded the house. The police ordered the men inside to surrender. Two shots could be heard, both fired from upstairs by Jackson's partner. Then Griffo hit the front door. The camera showed his back as he went in and went down in a spray of bullets.

The other officers rushed in and shot Jackson and collected his partner. Griffo was dead and Jackson wasn't, although he probably wished he was, because several cops were so distraught they beat and kicked Jackson within view of the camera. Suddenly, the taping ended.

That videotape made Jackson famous. It put him on the evening news and the national news. It was shown so many times, even Geraldo Rivera ran out of commentary. Viewers probably stopped paying attention. The jury paid close attention.

Although the audio portion was poor, the video was compelling, like a jerky newsreel where you can't quite believe what you're seeing, because you're watching another human being getting shot to death. Griffo went through the door and went down. You couldn't see the shooter, but, seconds later, there was Jackson getting roughed up. The nine-millimeter Uzi knockoff with a twenty-five-round magazine was next to him, bearing his fingerprints. Five of the ten bullets it fired went into Griffo, and his bullet-proof vest became moot when two of them ripped through his skull.

The camera memorialized Griffo's bravery and his demise. The camera sealed Jackson's fate as well. Other officers testified they heard Jackson yell, 'You're a dead man!' Although the words weren't captured on tape, they weren't needed.

If the dictionary had an illustration for 'open and shut,' Jackson's picture would be appropriate. Game, set, and match. Turn the channel. It wasn't a question of a black man shooting a white man. A criminal had virtually executed a cop face to face, and no one wanted to rally in his behalf.

No one could claim Jackson didn't have adequate representation. His lawyer was a silver fox named Jerusalem Sterne, an eighty-year-old legend who knew every nest in the judicial henhouse. Jerusalem Sterne came up with the defense that his client had been getting ready to surrender. When the front door burst open it surprised and rattled Jackson so much, the gun went off unintentionally. As for shots being fired right before that, they came from upstairs. Manslaughter, or reckless homicide at worst.

Sterne also made much of the fact that the defendant had no history of violence, resistance, or hatred of the police. The defendant had spent a good part of his life stealing at gunpoint, but never used the gun, even to strike someone. Sterne's defense was so good it took the jury nearly four hours to return with guilty verdicts. By the time Jackson arrived on death row, Jerusalem Sterne was dead of a heart attack. Other lawyers would handle the usual appeals. Various appellate courts carefully mulled the facts and legal issues, and found no reason to reverse. Figuratively and literally, Jackson was on his way to a dead end.

Griffo became a symbol of police heroism. To serve and protect, he gave his life. His picture was added to the roll of honor in the lobby of headquarters. They named a boys' club after him, and a group of businessmen created a scholarship in his honor. At each stage of the appeals process his widow appeared to remind the hearing officer or judge of her husband's sacrifice.

I remembered most of this from the news coverage. What I didn't know or had forgot I found in the papers Kit had sent up from downtown. There were two stacks, each more than a foot deep. Except for an hour rewriting a will, I spent the remainder of the afternoon and most of the evening reading testimony and pleadings. I found nothing to change my opinion about anything. Although Kit was having the tape analyzed using technology unavailable at the time of the trial, chances of seeing or hearing anything new were remote.

By the time I finished, bleary-eyed, past midnight, only one thing bothered me — Johnny Griffo's name. I had that name stored away in some remote niche of memory, and I didn't know where or why. I had the vague feeling someone had told me something about Griffo a long time ago, maybe in the days when I worked as a public defender in the gladiatorial pit known as the police courts.

In the morning I overslept, so I had to forego my usual run. I drank coffee and listened to Meg's voice on the recorder. Then I put on my tan khaki suit, button-down powder-blue shirt, comfortable beige walking shoes, and my best red tie, and drove downtown in the creeping gauntlet of rush-hour traffic.

The AUL building was located a couple of blocks from what the city modestly called the Crossroads of America. That it was built and financed by an insurance company says a lot about our downtown. The white tower symbolized stability and conservatism. If you walked into the lobby wearing anything other than some version of a corporate uniform, the security guards tended to pay more attention and other people gave you that secret look of appraisal. No one paid any attention to me on the crowded elevator. I was one of them.

In Indy, you can't get much higher than the Skyline Club, unless you're in a helicopter. The location has as much to do with status as altitude. Privacy and privilege come together in the club, which has its own floor just above my father's law firm. From the tables overlooking the city, the movers and shakers do a good deal of their moving and shaking, or so I've been told. To update an old line, I wouldn't belong to any club that wouldn't have me as a member, and the Skyline Club wouldn't have me as a member. No problem. I couldn't afford it anyway.

I was late, which was a little galling because it gave Larry Lynch some private moments with Kit. Larry was the governor's chief of staff and a friend of sorts, more of Kit than me, from our days in law school. I didn't like Larry for several hundred reasons. He was one of those golden boys whose thick blond hair was always perfectly styled. After an hour of tennis not a strand was out of place. And he had a dynamite serve. With his handsome Nordic features, Larry also looked good in sweaters, especially when he casually draped his sweater over his shirt. I hated that, because men only looked like that in *Esquire* ads.

Worse, Larry was a right-wing Republican. A good-looking, unmussable, right-wing Republican. As if all of this wasn't bad enough, he had had several dates with Kit in school. Luckily, Kit decided he was too perfect for a mere woman.

They had a corner table with a spectacular view of part of downtown, buildings of all sizes, shapes, and colors with wisps of morning mist painted around them. As I approached, Larry was touching Kit's elbow and laughing at some remark, probably one of his own.

He feigned enthusiasm. 'Ah, Mr Ritter. Long time no see. Sit down, sit down.'

'I ordered toast and coffee for you,' Kit said. 'Larry's been telling me about his daughter.' She sipped coffee and smiled at Lynch. 'To think you have three children.'

Larry tucked a snapshot in his wallet without bothering to show it to me. I noticed he had had a haircut, probably yesterday, and his nails were manicured. His double-breasted charcoal suit was impeccably tailored and without a trace of lint. Kit wore a beige suit with padded shoulders; her purse matched her black patent leather heels. To my eye, her hair had more of a honey tone than yesterday. Her chandelier earrings had tiny clusters of baby pearls.

'And what about you, Kit?' Larry said. 'Still dating that doctor? Ever going to get married?'

'You never know,' said Kit. 'Certainly not right away. I'm not worried about the biological clock.'

'The doc and I serve on several of the same boards,' Larry said. 'I told him we're old friends. I took my legal training into the shadowy world of politics; you took yours into the shadowy world of corporate law.' He raised an eyebrow. 'Katherine, my dear, how in the name of goodness did you come to represent a cop killer?'

'The firm wants to expand our criminal specialty. This is a good case, from a visibility standpoint.'

'Well, you're going to lose, so consider that.' He looked at his gold watch. 'Speaking of biological clocks, I have to move this along, because I have to be at a budget meeting.' He stared at me rather than Kit. 'You understand, this is strictly off-the-record. Sam Colson is the governor's E.A. for corrections. I'm just here to listen.'

A waiter in a tuxedo jacket began delivering the food. I sipped coffee and let Kit do the talking.

'We just want a fair shot,' she said. 'I'll be sending a clemency petition to the parole board. I don't expect them to be particularly sympathetic, but I would like a level playing field. We're short of options.'

'Why don't you think you'd get a fair hearing?'

'Because this is an election year. Because your boss has been working hard to get the support from law enforcement he didn't get before. Because private phone calls can be made. Because Jackson killed a policeman.'

Larry finished a mouthful of eggs Benedict.

'Dear, dear Kit. How cynical you've become. The governor appoints the board. He doesn't tell them how to vote. They are four fine, independent people. Any one of them, I'm sure, would resent interference.'

'Maybe the governor doesn't tell them personally,' I said, 'but I'm sure he has his ways of getting word out.'

'What about the Supreme Court?' Larry asked Kit rather than me. 'I mean the state court.'

'We're petitioning again,' Kit said, 'not that it'll do any good. We're petitioning the U.S. Supreme, but I doubt we'll even get to first base. That means clemency is our best chance, maybe our only chance. I'd like it to be a fair and honest chance.'

'A fair and honest chance, like Jackson gave that police officer?'

I said, 'One barbaric act by a cornered criminal shouldn't be matched by a similar barbaric act by a supposedly civilized government.'

'Excuse me, *Carson*,' Larry fired back, knowing the use of my given name would rankle me. 'I believe the highest court of this supposedly civilized country has embraced capital punishment. I believe polls consistently show a majority of citizens of this supposedly civilized country support the death penalty, especially in situations where a sworn officer of the law is needlessly massacred by a career criminal.'

'Yeah,' I said, 'and I believe that more than sixty countries have abolished the death penalty in the last decade.'

Kit intervened. 'Guys, please. We didn't come here to argue policy or philosophy.'

Larry arched an eyebrow. 'To my recollection, Kit, you were a pretty gung-ho prosecutor. Care to explain the switch?'

Kit shook her head no. 'Not if you're in such a hurry. Look, Larry, all we're asking for is a hands-off policy with the board. If they turn us down on the merits, they turn us down. I don't want to be swept out the door because the governor told his appointees he needs police votes.'

'The governor would never do such a thing,' said Larry. 'All right. I'll talk to Sam. Unofficially. If I hear anything . . . '

Kit patted his hand. 'I knew I could count on you.'

Larry wiped his mouth with a linen napkin.

'Let me give you kids a word of advice. I looked at the file. Jackson's lost at every step. Every conceivable argument has been proffered, to no avail. You know how many people have called, written, or e-mailed us in Jackson's behalf? Nobody. Zero. Nada.'

'So we should just back off?' I said.

'Sonny, Kit, don't you go to the movies? The poor guy on death row always has something going for him. He's a songwriter or an armless cripple. Or he's got a sweet wife and ten adorable kids. So what do we have with Jackson?' He started counting on his fingers. 'Criminal. Unmarried. Drug user. Literate, or literate enough. Doesn't write poetry or freedom songs. Shot a cop five times in front of a camera. Isn't especially repentant. In short, you're riding a loser.'

Kit smiled through gritted teeth. 'You have a gift for pointing out the obvious, dear Larry.'

'I've got to run. Good luck to you. So long, Sonny.'

Kit and I sat in silence after he left.

'Larry hasn't changed a bit,' I finally said. 'I still don't trust him.'

'You mean you don't like him. You haven't liked him since he placed second in the class.'

'I don't like him because he shellacs his hair.'

'We're lucky to have him on our side.'

'On our side? Kit, the only side Larry's on is his own. Even if Jackson had children who looked like the Von Trapp family, Larry could care less.'

'What I meant is at least he can keep the

governor's office neutral. Little as it is, it's something.' She looked at her watch. 'Are you going to talk to Jackson today?'

'I am going to talk to Jackson. After I stop off in Dodge City.' I frowned. 'Where the hills are alive with the sound of gunfire.'

6

Dodge city was the nickname of an inner-city area the chamber of commerce somehow omitted from its brochures. Crack cocaine reigned as king on its mean streets and alleys, gangs were the royal enforcers, and guns the principal means of enforcement.

At night, in nicer areas of the city, mosquitoes and fireflies filled the air; in Dodge City, only the bullets had wings. The odd thing was, the neighborhood was only a few blocks from the world's largest museum for children. There, kids could walk through a fantasy world of dinosaurs, sorcerers, and magic. In Dodge City, though, children faced danger far worse than any dragon. Here the kids grew up quickly, if they grew up at all.

Many of the homes were once impressive, three-story structures with huge porches, gables, turrets, and wedding-cake trim, built in the James Whitcomb Riley era. These days they were threadbare, decrepit, and forlorn, most whites having long ago fled to the suburbs. If he lived there now the Hoosier poet wouldn't go out at night, and Little Orphan Annie would be a tracked-up junkie turning tricks in the alley.

Yet Jeremiah Jackson's mother lived in a gray two-story cottage house remarkable for its neatness. Flowers lined the fenced-in yard, and the lawn had been edged. The white-and-green plastic chairs and small tables on the front porch were arranged like a window display. A sign on the door said WELCOME TO OUR HOME. As I waited for someone to respond to my knock, I noticed there were other houses like this, bright brave havens between places badly in need of paint, putty, and plaster.

When no one answered I opened the side gate and walked to the back. Beyond the lawn there was a long garden filled with rows of vegetables, mostly corn and tomatoes. An elderly black woman stood leaning on a cane and watching a black man pull weeds from the ground. The man's face glistened in the morning heat. His sleeves were rolled up, and I noticed his black shirt had a minister's collar.

'Good morning,' I said. 'My name is Sonny Ritter. I'm an attorney working with Katherine Lake.'

The woman reached out for my hand. Hers was warm and bony, twisted by arthritis, but her grip was like iron.

'Thank you, Mr Ritter,' she said in a

wheezy voice. 'Jesus sent you to save my son. I will add you to my prayer list.'

As near as I could tell, Mrs Jackson was close to eighty. Her stringy gray hair was sealed in a net and leathery creases lined her face. Her eyes were dark and sad. She wore a simple black dress, and her feet were encased in well-worn carpet slippers.

The man stood up and wiped his hands. He had wavy black hair and a handsome clipped moustache. His voice had a resonant bass.

'I'm the Reverend Foster, Melba's spiritual leader.'

'My strong right hand,' said Mrs Jackson. 'Please, come in to the house. It's cooler inside.'

In the living room all the furniture was old but seemingly in good condition. Plastic covered the sofa, the two stuffed chairs, and all of the lamps. Over the fireplace was an assortment of family photos, all of them in black and white. The other walls had religious paintings, mostly of New Testament scenes.

I sat on the sofa as the minister and Jackson's mother occupied the chairs.

'Miss Lake, she is a *wonderful* attorney,' Mrs Jackson said, bobbing her head. 'And she's such a *nice* lady. I pray for her every day. I'll pray for you, too, Mr Ritter.'

'Thank you, ma'am.'

'This dear lady is a lighthouse,' Foster said with a nod towards Mrs Jackson. 'Nothing can turn out her beacon. You may not know it, but you followed the light here.'

'Well,' I started, groping for words that wouldn't be too hurtful, 'I'm here for several reasons. Perhaps the most important one is to let Mrs Jackson know that while she should be optimistic, she also needs to be realistic. We're doing what we can, but . . . '

'What exactly are you doing?' the minister said. He wiped his neck and brow with a handkerchief.

'I'm re-examining the facts, mainly. Miss Lake will handle most of the legal issues. Don't get me wrong, she's the best you can get. But, you see . . . '

Foster shook his head. 'This woman here, this good woman, raised a thousand dollars for J.J. Do you have any idea how much a thousand dollars is to someone like her? It's a million dollars. She sold baked goods. She babysat. She sacrificed. She begged. Please, I understand what you're trying to say, but don't say it was for nothing.'

I probably looked embarrassed. I felt embarrassed. But I had to press on.

'Mrs Jackson, in everything about this case over the years, everything you've seen or heard, is there anything you think has been neglected, overlooked, any salient point in your son's favor?'

'No sir,' she said without hesitating. 'But I believe in my boy. I believe what my son tells me. He didn't mean to kill that officer. He didn't want to kill that man. We all have to forgive, you know.'

'Now, at any time, did anyone come to you, did anyone call you, did someone say to you anything about the circumstances that didn't coincide with the testimony, the official version of the case? What I mean is, a stranger, a phone call, a letter, anything.'

'No, nothing.'

'Then did J.J. or his friends raise anything unusual, any suggestion or possibility . . . '

'No.'

I had groped as far as I dared. If his mother knew of any angle, however remote, that had been raised over the last eight years outside the official record, she didn't remember.

I felt uncomfortable. I really had come here to make sure this poor old woman was ready to face the inevitable. Now I realized I had no right to take away whatever sliver of hope she clung to.

'What about Tyrone?' I asked. 'What can you tell me about him?'

Tyrone Mason was Jackson's criminal

partner. He had pleaded guilty, cooperated with the police, and received a life sentence, without possibility of parole. Then he cheated the state. Mason was HIV positive, and four years after landing in prison, he developed full-blown AIDS. He had been sent home to die.

'He was a bad influence on J.J.,' Mrs Jackson said. 'Even though he refuses to embrace Jesus, I do believe he's finally making his way to heaven, amen.'

'Amen,' Foster said.

I said, 'Can you give me the names of any of J.J.'s friends, that is, people he was running around with at the time, that perhaps no one else has talked to? A girlfriend or wife, say.'

'J.J. didn't bring the ladies home. He knew better than that. As for friends, well, I'm sorry to say they were bad people. It's the drugs, you see. You know who sells the drugs? The devil sells the drugs. Children buy the drugs and don't know the devil's buying them as he sells, don't you see.'

She moved her finger to signal me to come closer. As I did so, she took a photo album from the lamp stand at her side. I knelt next to her. There was an array of pictures showing a handsome, bright-eyed boy wearing a Catholic school uniform, wearing a Cub Scout uniform, riding a bicycle with training wheels, and always smiling.

'Does that look like the face of a killer?' she whispered. 'I didn't raise my boy to be no killer.'

'I'm sure you didn't, Mrs Jackson.'

'Lord, it's hot today,' Foster said. 'Come on, Mr Ritter. I'll walk you to your car.'

Mrs Jackson shook my hand with both of hers, as if she somehow could transfer her certainty to me.

The neighborhood was almost slow-motion quiet. From behind the fence next door three little black girls stopped playing so they could stare at the two giants who came into view, one black and one white.

I could see their clothes, shoes, and toys, all probably from second-hand stores or church bazaars, and I saw the dilemma of the modern city. In the suburbs, the kids were mostly white and the houses mostly new, and the clothes were new and the toys were new and the schools were new, or at least not old. Here everything was used. Yet some of the poor families in these once-beautiful homes now were being displaced because whites with money were tired of driving back and forth to the suburbs.

The minister patted me on the shoulder as we approached my car.

'Bless you for coming like this. You wanted

to tell Mrs Jackson the truth when you didn't have to. You're a good man. I know you're going to do your best.'

'I'm going to talk to J.J. Will you be there for the . . . '

He exhaled emotion as well as air. 'Oh, yes. I'm his spiritual counselor. His mother's ready, you know. She knows Jeremiah will be with Jesus eventually.'

'You know J.J. pretty well, don't you? You've talked to him privately, many times.'

'Yes, I have. Did he confess something to me he wouldn't tell anyone else? No.'

'What about Tyrone Mason?'

The weight of some memory bowed the minister's head.

'Truth be told, the man's always been godless. Doesn't believe in anything. Wouldn't listen to anybody. The devil had both hands on Tyrone's heart. Then he got AIDS. Got it, I expect, from one of his ladies. I thought this would change him, but it didn't. Man's heart was hardened. But, you know, the farther down they are, the longer God's arm reaches.'

'Do you ever see Mason?'

'Oh, yes. Saw him the other day. At his sister's house. Looks like he's dead. I'm afraid, though, he isn't.'

'You've talked about the day of the shooting?'

'Yes, indeed. Why didn't he just give up? Why did he shoot at the police?' Foster's involuntary laugh carried a hint of scorn. 'Because he wanted to scare them, so he and J.J. could escape out the back door! Can you believe the sheer stupidity? That's what the boy said. I don't have to tell you he isn't the smartest creature ever to walk God's green earth.'

'Did Mason see anything when the police brought him downstairs?'

'If he did he wouldn't say. Believe Tyrone was pretty scared by then, and the police beat him up before they brought him outside.'

'Was Mason a product of his environment? This neighborhood?'

'Yes, but please, don't blame the neighborhood.' He swept his hand through the air to cover all directions. 'Quiet right now, isn't it? Kids playing. Woman pushing her baby in a carriage. Cars go by, bet you drivers worry about getting a flat. Don't want to stop in Dodge City, do they?'

'I don't suppose so.'

'This is a bad place, I don't have to tell you that. But some rise out of the ashes. We've had children who've become very successful, business people, lawyers like you, pillars in many pursuits. J.J., well, to tell the truth, he could have walked the righteous path, and he turned his back. Even when he was a teenager he always had this criminal streak in him. Must have got it from his daddy, who disappeared before he could walk. But he was just greedy, not violent.'

'Reverend, what did he tell you about that day?'

'Said he didn't mean to kill Officer Griffo. I believed him. Still believe him.'

'But he did pull the trigger?'

'Yes, I'm afraid he did.'

7

It's hard to drive through the flatlands of northwestern Indiana without thinking of a sinister crop-dusting plane chasing Cary Grant across a cornfield. Alfred Hitchcock knew how to manipulate his audiences, how to use the camera to mislead the eye. That stark Indiana cornfield, for instance, wasn't even filmed in Indiana. Who could tell the difference? No one.

The three-hour drive up north gave me time to think, and I thought about the BBC videotape. Did the camera force the eye to see one thing to the exclusion of another? In a handful of seconds we saw Griffo force the front door open, move through the doorway, stop, move slightly backwards, and, peppered by bullets, collapse. Was there something we didn't see? Well, we couldn't see Jeremiah Jackson. Still, we couldn't see the bullets either, but we knew they were there.

The videotape had been used to help convict Jackson. I wondered if there was some way it could be used to help save him. I wondered, too, whether he deserved to be saved.

The state prison was located near Michigan City, a town about halfway between Chicago and South Bend. The first sight of the heavily wired perimeter and the somber buildings that looked like warehouses with bars always reminded me of why I became a lawyer. Here were civilization's most dangerous creatures, the psychopaths and sociopaths who preyed upon the rest of us and looked upon murder and rape in the same way a twisted child looked upon torturing a frog. Here were society's misfits, too, the thugs and thieves who did what they wanted and took what they wanted and had only an imprecise idea of why it was wrong. Here as well were the people I considered society's failures — the criminals of varying degrees who never got a break when they were kids, or were twisted by their own parents' abuse, or fell into a pattern of crime because the desperate need for drugs or alcohol blinded them to the other choices. I had come to believe that the law had a necessary and vital function, to protect us from each other, but also a magnificent societal role, to recognize and save the misguided and misbegotten who were worth saving if only someone cared enough to try to reach them before it was too late.

Visits to death row were different than visits with other inmates. The security was stricter, the paperwork more tedious, and the guards more vigilant. I waited nearly an hour in the spartan reception room before being escorted to see Jackson.

We went through a series of corridors and barred doors. Finally the guard opened a meshed door and led me through a metal detector. On the other side was nothing more than a large cage with a table and chairs. The whitened walls were bare except for a calendar and clock, reminders that here time ended when appeals ended.

Jackson wore white coveralls, tennis shoes, and handcuffs with enough slack to allow him to carry a folder and what looked like a law book. What surprised me was how old he looked. He was forty-five going on sixty-five. His hairless skull was as bare as a pecan shell but his eyebrows and goatee were the color of chalk. He had sleepy brown eyes and a scribble of a moustache, black with flakes of silver. He was shorter than I expected, maybe five-eight, probably quite strong for a man weighing around one-fifty, and the nails on his spindly fingers were unusually long and shiny, as if he buffed them every day.

We stared at each other across the rectangular metal table.

'My name is Sonny Ritter. I'm an attorney working with Katherine Lake.'

Jackson had a languid, smoky voice.

'Yeah. Quite a woman, her, if you know what I mean. Prettiest lawyer I ever seed. What you going to do that she ain't?'

'Ask you more questions about the shooting.'

Jackson had a way of starting his sentences with a kind of low chuckle, a barely audible heh-heh.

'Well, sir, I told the story so many times to so many peoples, I don't know where to start. Why don't you ask questions?'

'Fine. Let's start before then. The police had six warrants for armed robbery. Did you in fact commit those robberies?'

When Jackson opened his mouth this time, he flashed a gold tooth.

'In fact, I did. Shit, them and a lot more. Yes, sir, guilty.'

'Was the weapon you carried in those holdups the weapon that killed Sergeant Griffo?'

'Yes, it was. Sure was.'

'Uzi knockoff. Pretty heavy artillery if you're not going to use it.'

Jackson's expression of faint surprise suggested the point had shot right over my head, metaphorically speaking.

'That's exactly right. You show 'em a grease gun, brother, you don't *have* to use it.'

'I see. Now, the house. Your old girlfriend's house. She was at work. Did she tip off the police?'

'No, she didn't. See, it was T-Man's sister what did. T-Man, that's Tyrone Mason. She came up to the prison and fessed up to T, crying and what not. She told the pulleeses where we were on account of her boyfriend who was in trouble. Real sorry she was, cuz, you know, what happened.'

'Did you have any dealings or encounters with Sergeant Griffo before that day?'

'No, sir, I didn't. T-Man did. He knew the man. He knew, you know, his rep, his thing, you know what I'm saying?'

'Not exactly.'

'Heh-heh. Well, on the street, see, Sergeant Griffo and his partner, Buckley, Dickie Buckley, they were two bad-ass motherfuckers. See, they had a little thing they liked to do. Griffo liked to beat on you some. Buckley, he'd hold you. Beat the shit out of you just for kicks, you know what I'm saying?'

'How do you know this?'

'Well, like I say, cuz T-Man, he knew, cuz they beat him up. And other brothers, they knew the man. Stay out of the man's way, you know, cuz he's one bad ass.'

None of this had been in the trial

testimony. I said, 'Did you tell this to Mr Sterne?'

'Yes, sir, I did. I remember exactly what he told me, cuz there were four reasons to say nothing. Least he said they were reasons. First, let's see. Nobody's going to believe me. Second was, uh, no proof anyhow. Third, cuz the jury wouldn't like him, Mr Sterne, attackin' Sergeant Griffo's character. That's the word he used, character. And, uh, four, well, the jury might think I shot Sergeant Griffo cuz I was scared he was goin' to beat me.'

'Did you know it was Griffo outside?'

The gold tooth flashed, like a glass eye you could only notice when the light hit it a certain way, and his eyes shone with a hint of amusement.

'You know, I spent thirteen and a half years in prison. Before this, I mean. I spent lots of time on the streets. I been in fights, and I been beaten by pretty big peoples. Funny thing about a beatin'. Less you get your jaw broke or something, you be all right. I wasn't afraid of the pulleese *beatin'* me. I was afraid the motherfuckers was goin' to *shoot* me. Hell, I'd throw the guns out the door and let them kick the shit out of me for a week long as they don't kill me.' He showed a keyboard of teeth. 'See, I like livin', the girls and the drugs and such, you know.'

'Okay. You were downstairs and T-Man was upstairs.'

'Right, right. Smoked a little weed before. Working on our, you know, situation. And he yelled down the pulleeses were all around and it's that motherfucker Griffo and like an army or something. Tell you the truth, it scared the shit out of me. I looked out and it looked like what they call commandos, and they was comin' up the porch.'

'And then?'

Jackson's shoulders slumped. He shook his head, as if the memories stirred up demons for the first time.

'So fast, you know, like lightnin'. I just naturally grabbed the gun. Then I'm thinking, whoa, baby, they're gonna drive a fuckin' tank through the door. Then I heard 'pulleese.' Then two shots, pop, pop, from upstairs. The door come flyin' open and he's standing there pointin' a gun, like, you know, like he's gonna kill me.'

'And you yelled, 'You're a dead man.''

'That's what the officers said. But I didn't. That's what *he* yelled, Sergeant Griffo. They thought I did. But he did.'

'And?'

'Like it happened so fast. I kind of jerked the gun up, cuz he was gonna shoot me, and just, you know, the trigger, them guns, like a reaction. Bullets sprayin' all over. All in a second or two, you know what I'm saying?'

'I know what you're saying. I just have difficulty believing you. For instance, if Griffo came through the door and saw you standing there with a weapon, why didn't he shoot you? That's what any cop would do. Not that it makes any difference in my role, but I find your story rather hard to swallow.'

'Well, yeah, so did Mr Sterne. But, you know, I'm just tellin' you what happened, man.'

I had dealt with enough professional criminals to know lying was second nature for most of them. Jackson had told his story so many times, he probably believed it himself. One thing was clear. I would have to re-read Mason's statements and maybe ask Mason additional questions, if that was even possible.

Jackson and I stared at each other across the table. It was about two and a half feet wide, and wider than the Grand Canyon. Until the other night, I had never looked deep into the eyes of a man who was walking a short path to his own demise. I looked into Jackson's eyes and thought I saw the other side of midnight, just dark clouds and rocks and a gray bottomless sea.

'Well,' he said, 'anything more?'

'You can give me the names of anyone you think might have pertinent information. Your street friends, for instance, people you were running with at the time.'

'Don't have no names that knows nothin'. Just T-Man. Poor old T-Man, got the virus, make him look like a skeleton, and they wouldn't even let him out of here, 'cept'n when they carried him out in a ambulance while his sister cried.'

'I'm sorry. I'm sorry about your situation as well. I talked to your mother this morning. She's praying for you. She's certain you'll be going to heaven.'

A wan smile crossed Jackson's mouth.

'Yeah, well, they say you jus' close your eyes and go to sleep. Got some guards here, they remember the electric chair. Called it Hot Squat. They like to talk about it, like, you know, seein' guys cookin' like they was bacon in the fryin' pan and smoke coming from their heads and such. They say, 'You're a lucky boy. All they gonna do is stick a needle in you and you won't feel a thing.''

'If anyone can get a stay or commutation, Kit Lake can.'

'Yes, sir, I believe you're right. Prettiest lawyer I've ever had, that's for sure. Wished

I'd of had her instead of Mr Jerusalem Sterne.'

I picked up my legal pad.

'We all make choices we regret. How are you feeling? I mean really, about this . . . thing.'

For the first time, Jackson averted his eyes.

'Well, you know, I'm scared. I don't want to die. Guess none of us do. You know, I'm a thief but I ain't no killer.' A kind of sob came out. 'Other thing is, I gotta lot of things to account for. Things my mama don't know nothin' about.'

'I was in your mother's living room this morning. I knelt next to her and looked at pictures. I saw a cute kid who had a loving mother, good schooling, scouting, that kind of stuff. What happened to that kid? How'd he end up with so many things to account for?'

Jackson cleared his throat. 'I won't give you no bullshit answer. Won't blame the system, how we lived, my daddy bein' gone. Won't even blame the drugs. Tell you the truth, I just like easy money. Easy money, you know, for the cars and the booze and the ladies. Once you get a taste, you want another, see what I'm saying? Man, I did have me a taste, I surely did.'

It was, I thought, the most candid thing he

had said. But it wasn't the kind of comment calculated to melt anyone's heart. J.J. wasn't a prison poet, a symbol of justice off the tracks, a child gone wrong out of poverty, or a rallying point for minority rights or any other rights. He was just a criminal.

I said, 'Is there anything else I can do for you?'

'Yeah, there is. You know anything about gold?'

'Not really.'

He raised his upper lip. 'See this gold tooth? Might be worth some money. Like to make sure my mama gets it after, you know, after the thing.'

'I'll see what I can do,' I promised.

8

The morning heat was a toasty eighty degrees but not yet sticky. As I jogged northward along the edge of the boulevard, the sun slowly warmed the back of my cut-off T-shirt. By the time I worked up a light sweat, the shops of Broad Ripple had faded, like a movie set put into storage, and with it went civilization and its discontents. The river under the bridge was so shallow it looked like the water had been painted on.

With the help of federal money the city had converted an abandoned railroad line into a concrete jogging strip called the Morton Trail. I preferred the solitude of the roadside. I didn't mind the women in tight shorts, but bicyclists, roller-skating yuppies, and people trying to shrink beer bellies or cheeseburger butts distracted me.

Running laundered my mind. It washed out and dried the accumulated facts and memories, letting them tumble around in my brain without logic or purpose. The impact of my feet pounding along the ground next to the two-lane asphalt pavement somehow shot up to my head and awakened thoughts and ideas. It was as if I carried a box of puzzle pieces and running sometimes jolted them enough so several might fall into place.

I thought about J. J. Jackson. I replayed his words in hopes I'd hear something whose significance had slipped by me. I tried to think of some critical question I'd forgotten to ask. I journeyed eight years into the past, to a rundown house in a rundown neighborhood, and tried to follow the sequence of events leading to the death of Johnny Griffo. I sent his name back along the canyons of memory in the expectation that some sliver of information I couldn't remember would reappear, like a file card stuck to the back of another card.

Nothing worked. I ran two miles out and two back, and ended up showering and dressing with the same questions.

At my office I listened to my special message from Meg, called Kit and left a message, and spent a couple of hours reading police interviews and trial testimony. Just before ten, I telephoned the late Jerusalem Sterne's old office to arrange to see his files.

Kit returned my call right after I hung up.

'You made quite an impression with Jackson,' I said. 'Quite a package, Jeremiah is. If they had baseball cards for criminals, he'd be a hot ticket.'

'Not exactly the poster child for the anti-capital punishment lobby,' Kit agreed. 'I prosecuted more Jeremiah Jacksons than I care to remember.'

'And I've had a hundred clients just like him. He's the first I've met on death row. Cheery place.'

'I'm convinced life without the possibility of parole is the appropriate penalty, Sonny. He probably would have got life if he shot a civilian instead of a police officer.'

'If he shot a civilian he'd probably be out on parole. Jackson did bring up a couple of interesting things we can chew on. When can we get together?'

'We're having our final strategy session this afternoon. I'd like you to sit in, but Professor Meek's going to be there, and you two don't get along. If you can come down around noon, we can have lunch before the meeting. I'll meet you in the cafeteria.'

'You're the boss, boss.'

When I hung up, I suddenly realized how much I trusted Kit, because few other law school contemporaries had managed to get this far in their careers without having their outlook hardened if not poisoned by the criminal justice system. That's just the way she was, good-natured and blessed with the intelligence and confidence to keep from being contaminated. Some of the credit belonged to her father, a long-time judge with an impeccable reputation, and her mother, the principal of a private school who had made career and family seem like they were part of the same thing. Kit had wonderful genes. She also looked wonderful in jeans, another reason why she always made my puppytail wag. I worried about her, though. I didn't want her to be hurt when the state sent J.J. Jackson down that one-way corridor to the underworld from which there is no return.

I spent an hour preparing a quitclaim deed for a client who was moving to Florida. When I finished I dropped a copy off at his house, accepted his small check and thanks, and headed downtown.

Maybe a hundred people were eating lunch in the AUL building's main floor cafeteria. Kit was easy to find. All I had to do was triangulate the gazes of the men who were trying not to be obvious as they stared at her. A tall, strawberry-blonde woman who has a madonna's face and a model's grace tends to make hungry males sitting nearby spill goulash on their ties.

I didn't stare at Kit or any other woman seated along the periphery of the cavernous dining hall. I stared at the woman sharing the table with Kit. She was thirty-two, five feet tall, weighed one hundred pounds, had thin hair the color of a sun-drenched cornfield, and round red-rimmed glasses. She liked gardening, classical music, long walks, and amusement parks. She had a strawberry birthmark the size of my thumb on her right hip. Her name was Meg.

'Surprise, surprise,' I said, too surprised to think of anything better.

'Hi, Sonny,' Meg said. 'How are you?'

She had been my companion, girlfriend, lover, and wife, and seeing her in the flesh for the first time in months gave me a jolt. What I was thinking was, 'How could we hurt each other the way we did?' What I wanted to say was, 'Oh, baby, let's forget this ever happened.' What I said was, 'I'm fine, Meg. It's good to see you.'

'I'm glad you're working with Kit, Sonny. I'm glad your practice is starting to come back.'

I stood there awkwardly and heard myself say, 'It'll take time. That's one thing I have a lot of. How are your dad and mom?'

'They're fine. Debbie's going to dental school.'

'Good for her, good for her.'

'Well, I'd better get back upstairs,' Meg said. 'Good luck on the Jackson appeal, you two.'

'Thanks. Take care.'

Kit watched me as I watched Meg carry her tray away.

'Sorry,' she said. 'It was coincidence. You're seldom at a loss for words.'

'I seldom get the opportunity to revisit my train wreck. Excuse me.'

I caught up with Meg as she passed the gift shop on her way to the elevators.

'Hey, don't rush off. I want to ask you a question.'

She turned and faced me in a way that reminded me of how she had worked on her posture, how we used to ride bikes to keep in shape, how I had to teach her to swim because she was afraid of the water. An entire reel of memories played in my mind in the second I tried to think of something to say.

'What is it, Sonny?'

'That dress. Is that a new dress? I don't remember buying that dress for you.'

I didn't see the dress. I saw the naked shoulders under the fabric, the freckles on her back, the way her skin would dimple when she folded her legs, a thousand flashes from the past.

'You didn't. It's new.'

'Well, it's a nice dress. You look very nice in it.'

'Thank you.' Was there a subatomic

fracture in the iceberg of her voice?

'It's great seeing you, kid. Miss you. Take care of yourself.'

'Goodbye, Sonny.'

And so she was gone.

When I returned to the table Kit stared at me with an arched eyebrow. 'Maybe you'd like to get some food before we talk.'

Remembering things I had tried to forget, I went through the line and got a sandwich and coffee and brought them to Kit's table. She was scribbling notes on a legal pad.

'You okay?'

'Yeah,' I said. 'The bleeding's stopped. A little nourishment and I'll be as good as new. I may need a little of your nursing.'

'Sonny, you're incorrigible. One moment you're wounded from seeing your ex-wife, the next moment the wolf's starting to crawl through your eyeballs. *Men*.'

'It's not our fault. It's the curse of the penis. Imagine how much smoother things would be in this world if women had them. Come to think of it, some of them do.'

The image amused me, though in truth I was trying to hide behind wit so I didn't have to think about the chain reaction of emotions just seeing Meg for one minute started.

I could see Kit didn't share my humor.

'Sorry. Uncalled for. To business. What's

happening on the legal front?'

This was one of the rare times when Kit's face showed strain. The shadows under her aqua-blue eyes told of late hours and not enough sleep. She wore a khaki-colored pants suit with a pale violet blouse, accented by a dark violet belt and scarf.

'Just a final quarterbacking session to make sure we've covered all the stops,' she said. 'Our petitions are on the way to the Supreme Court. The professor's came up with a computer study of the racial makeup of the jury compared to other juries at the time. I think it has some merit.'

'It'll barely get over the transom before they throw it back.'

Kit nodded bleakly. 'Probably. We're taking the same approach with the Indiana Supreme Court. We'll probably get the same result. That's why I've been concentrating on the clemency petition. I think it's pretty good.'

'No parole board in the history of this state has ever recommended commuting a capital sentence.'

'There's supposed to be a first time for everything. I've got J.J.'s prison record. He really has been a model prisoner. That might count for something.'

'What else?'

'The videotape analysis. Four minutes of

tape now takes nearly an hour to watch. I didn't see anything startling. I had two of the interns watch it, and they saw what everybody else sees. Anyway, you and I need to go over it together. I'm not sure when I'll have the time. Maybe tomorrow.'

'At your service. What else?'

Kit shook her head and made a sour face. 'Nothing else. Sorry if I sound cranky. I'm doing a lot of this at night. What have you got?'

'Our client had one interesting wrinkle. He says Tyrone Mason and others of his ilk told him Griffo liked to beat people up.'

'Even if true, does it have any relevance? And how do you prove it?'

'It might have had relevance at trial. Eight years later, I doubt it. Sterne apparently didn't want to bring it up before the jury because he thought they might see it as a motive for J. J. Or so Jackson says.'

'Maybe we can have Jackson take a polygraph test.'

'Waste of time. Anyway, I don't trust lie detectors. Like guitars, they depend too much on the player. Really good liars and sociopaths can beat them. Put Jackson on one and he'd sound like Eric Clapton. Besides, nobody's going to admit a poly at the last hour.'

'I suppose you're right. Anything else?'

'Yeah. Jackson says he never said, 'You're a dead man.' Griffo said it, not him.'

Kit bobbed her head. 'He told me the same thing. I've been trying to think of a reason why he would lie about it. Or, if he's telling the truth, why two officers would lie about it.'

'When Griffo came through the door and saw J. J's gun, I doubt that he was throwing out one-liners. Again, though, what difference does it make? Even if we could persuade the police to say they were mistaken, it wouldn't by itself constitute fundamental error.'

'But would raise the question of what else they were mistaken about,' Kit countered. 'Or, conversely, raise the question of why Jackson would lie when there's no reason to.' She sighed, signaling frustration as much as anything. 'He's had a lot of time to remember things differently. But then you would think if he's going to change his story, he'd come up with something better. He's not smart, but he's not dumb, either. Where do you go next?'

'Try to talk to Mason, I guess. Also Sterne's office is going to dig up his original file. I know what he put in the record, but not what he didn't put in.'

'Like a note, a police report, a phone number, anything Sterne didn't think was important enough to pursue. You might as well buy a lottery ticket while you're at it.'

'Remember, the man liked his bottle. I think he was probably better at trial than preparing for trial. I also want to take a look at Griffo's personnel file. Maybe there'll be some telltale complaints. I'm also going to check in with the *Chronicle* reporter who covered the trial.'

'I'm doing all the boring stuff,' Kit said. 'You're having all the fun.' She glanced at her watch. 'I'd better get upstairs.'

'Tell Meg how glad I was to see her, will you?'

9

Tyrone Mason had been released from prison so he could die in his sister's home.

Don't think the department of corrections let him go out of the goodness of its big bureaucratic heart. The department was glad not to have to deal with the expensive medical difficulties of caring for an inmate who was not much more than a living corpse. The department preferred to have healthy, functioning inmates like Jeremiah Jackson, whom it could kill on a precise, tidy bureaucratic schedule.

Sadly, Mason's fate was not that different from that of the inner-city neighborhood that produced him. I looked through my windshield at a landscape on life support, stricken with an urban disease that appeared fatal. The open sores of the slow death were everywhere. They showed up as broken curbs and cracked sidewalks and vacant lots overrun with weeds. The facades of the paint-chipped houses had long ago been quarantined to prevent the spread of infection. Here, the broken glass of gin bottles and the alleys with discarded hypodermic needles were far from benign. In the daytime, the neglect was just as apparent as the heat and humidity, but it remained long after the sun went down.

The city had cleaned up part of College Avenue, but like the other kind of jungle where wild animals roam, the rot began returning as soon as the cleaning crews left. There was nothing really to stop it. The people hanging around the variety store didn't care, the people coming and going from the liquor stores didn't see, and the handsome models in the several billboards were preoccupied smoking soothing cigarettes or sipping delicious tropical cocktails. Certainly most of the motorists were indifferent; they were looking for hookers, scoring drugs, or cruising through on their way to better neighborhoods, their view limited by symbolic blinders.

Where Mrs Jackson's well-kept residence was one of several havens in Dodge City, the Mason place was a tired rust-colored house of one story with a screened porch and plastic sheets over most of the visible windows. The fat-finned 1955 Cadillac parked on blocks in the driveway looked like some relic that had crashed through a time warp. Most of the other houses on the block were vacant; one had a condemned sign, but I could see two men sitting on the ground sharing a bottle in a bag.

I knocked and waited. From inside loud voices shouted at each other. When no one answered, I banged with my fist. A few minutes later, a woman's face peered through the screen door.

'What you want?'

'I'm an attorney working for the Jackson family. I want to talk to Tyrone, if that's possible.'

'T'ain't. Go away.'

'J.J. asked me to give T-Man a message. Very important.'

She was a huge woman, maybe three hundred pounds, probably in her thirties. She had very dark skin and a slight moustache. She was wearing a black blouse, cut-off jeans, and thongs. She examined me for a full thirty seconds.

'Tyrone can't talk. Give me the message.'

'Do you mind if I come in for a minute? I sure can use a glass of water.'

She considered this for twenty seconds, and unlatched the door.

I handed her my card. 'I'm Sonny Ritter. And you are?'

'Darling, Darling Mason. T's sister.'

She turned indifferently, and I followed her inside. The living room was a cramped, cluttered space notable for two big stuffed sofas, two gaudy paintings of parrots, two large electric fans going full blast, and a giant-screen color TV broadcasting a game show with the sound loud enough to make Metallica get earplugs.

Darling sank her large self into one of the sofas and began watching TV as if I had evaporated.

I planted myself in the other sofa. 'Can you turn the TV down for a minute?'

'What?'

'Can you turn the TV down?'

'No.'

Even with the fans it was probably ninety degrees in the room. I got up and turned the sound off but left the picture on. Darling didn't protest. She dropped her head back and waited for me to say something.

I said, 'I read your brother's police statements and testimony. I'd like to know if anything happened he didn't tell anybody about.'

'Why?'

'The state's getting ready to execute J.J. If there's any information that might help him, I'd like to know before it's too late. How is Tyrone, by the way?'

'Bad.'

We sat there staring at each other.

'It must be tough taking care of a sick brother,' I said after a minute. 'You must love your brother a lot.'

The remark seemed to make a connection. She bit her lip.

'It ain't easy. So many peoples lied to me. They said Tyrone'd be dead in three or four months. He ain't dead. He just sick. He wishes he be dead. Be better off, anyway.'

'Do you have any nursing help?'

'Couldn't get along without it. Meals on wheels, too. Only ones who come here. T's friends, they don't come. Scared they'll get the bug, you know.'

'Miss Mason . . . Darling . . . is there anything your brother told you about the shooting that didn't come out before? What I mean is, something that perhaps the authorities didn't want people to know. I'm sorry, I can't be more specific.'

'Tyrone got life even though J.J. shot that man. T didn't. J.J. shot him. Now they're gonna kill J.J. I don't know what you mean, mister. All Tyrone wanted to talk about was that fucking bitch who gave him AIDS. Bitch knew she had it and didn't tell him.'

'Was he able to track down the woman? So others could be warned?'

Darling shook as she made a cackling sound. '*I* tracked the bitch down. Know where I found her? New Crown Cemetery. Deader than shit, and just turned thirty. Say, what's this message from J.J.?'

'If you don't mind, I'd like to tell Tyrone myself.'

'Well, he can't talk.'

'He can hear, can't he?'

Her nod told me he could. With a lugubrious sigh, she lifted herself from the sofa. 'Back here,' she said.

I followed her along the creaky floor of a hallway to a back bedroom. It was like walking into a greenhouse. The room had the faint reek of rancid food. The air was so stale I felt like I was breathing through a gas mask. A bed sheet hung over the only window, blocking the light and the view. The room had a single metal-frame bed, a card table with folding legs, some medical equipment, and a portable TV offering the same game show Darling had been watching.

Mason lay in the bed, covered up to his chin by a sheet. A wire ran from the TV to the earphones on his head. He didn't move at all, even when his sister removed the earphones.

He was alive, but he was dead, too. His face was emaciated and shrunken like a coconut. The hair and beard were white as ashes. The skin dripped with perspiration. From the shape of his body, he looked like he didn't weigh more than sixty or seventy pounds. I could see enough of his arm to observe where the IV was inserted. At the side of his bed was an oxygen unit, not in use at the moment.

His sister said, 'Tyrone, this is J.J.'s lawyer. Got a message from J.J.'

Mason didn't blink or otherwise move.

I stood there uncomfortably, trying to think of a message as I realized Mason was beyond helping anyone, especially himself.

'Hello, Tyrone,' I said. 'I just talked to J.J. He wants you to know how sorry he is about what's happened to you. He wants you to know he's been thinking about you.'

Mason gave no indication of hearing anything. The eyes stared straight ahead, two shiny brown marbles looking down that one-way path leading to infinity.

'Well,' his sister said. 'Ain't that something?'

'Can he hear us all right?'

'Oh, yeah. Nothing wrong with his hearing. Just can't talk or nothing. Can't hardly move a'tall.'

I stepped closer to the bed.

'Tyrone, I read all your statements. Was there something you left out? Did anything happen you weren't supposed to tell?'

Again, no sign.

'Yeah,' Darling said. 'I can tell by his eyes.'

Mason made a kind of wheezing noise. I reached over and touched his wrist. The skin felt like dried-out paper ready to disintegrate.

'I didn't see anything,' I said.

'He talks with his eyes, mister.'

'You ask him. Ask him what I just asked him.'

Darling repeated the question. I thought I saw a faint change in Mason's eyes, and decided I was imagining it.

'Something,' Darling said. She turned back to her brother. 'Well, it's good to hear from J.J., ain't it? You watch TV now. Pretty soon I'll bring you some fresh water.'

We went back into the living room. She plopped into the sofa and let the fans sweep tepid air over her body.

'God, it's hot in there. But I think it's good for him. In the winter he was always cold. Heat's good for him.'

'When he could talk, when he could talk before this, did he ever talk about getting beat up by the police?'

'Uh-uh. Not with me he didn't. I didn't know, you know, what he was doing and all that. Fact I hadn't seen him for, I don't know, like a year before the thing, the shooting. He just called me, see. We ain't got no other family anyhow.'

It suddenly occurred to me that taking care of her dying brother was the woman's penance. Eight years ago, to help out her boyfriend, she had made the call that told the police where Jackson and Mason were hiding.

When I looked at her again I couldn't ask any more questions.

'Thanks for your time,' I said. 'I'll be leaving now.'

'The doctors said he'd be dead by now. It's a struggle every day. I mean to tell you, he'd be better off dead.'

'I'm sorry.'

I left this house of AIDS and drove out of the neighborhood that itself was slowly dying.

10

The seat of government in Indianapolis was a twenty-eight-story building buttressed between Law and Order. Law was the six-story west wing packed with courtrooms to process the work product of Order. Order was the six-story east wing containing the police department and the city jail. The personnel office directed me to the chief's office on the second floor.

When I told the polite, brown-haired receptionist I wanted to see Sergeant John Griffo's employment record, the half-dozen uniforms within earshot began staring at me.

'I'll have to see,' the receptionist said in a voice that also managed to say drop dead without using the words. She retreated towards a door leading to other offices. As I waited, the uniforms pretended to be busy as they prepared for act two.

Two minutes later, a lanky, balding man wearing wire-rim glasses strode up. He also wore the white shirt of rank and an expression approximating a junkyard dog trying to bite through a fence.

'I'm Lieutenant Rosenthal. What is it exactly that you want?'

'Sergeant Griffo's personnel file.'

All keyboards had ceased. All ears were perked up. Rosenthal stared at me as if I had just peed in a holy fountain. He was controlling himself, and he wanted me to see it.

'And you are?'

'Carson Ritter, attorney.'

Some people can speak volumes without uttering a word. What Rosenthal said via his face and body language communicated something about radical lawyers wanting to destroy the fabric of society.

He raised his voice so everyone could hear his speech.

'Since Sergeant Griffo . . . gave his life . . . in the service to the department, the community, and its citizens . . . his personnel file . . . has been archived. It'll take a day or two to locate it.'

I handed Rosenthal my card.

'Thanks. I'll be back in a day or two. Have a nice day.'

I had wanted to ask Mason for the names of any of his old street friends who might have been beaten by Griffo and Buckley, and couldn't. If any of the alleged victims had filed lawsuits, they wouldn't necessarily be easy to locate. I wondered if it would be worth the trouble to look. It would take a couple of hours to go through the court indexes, and even if I found something, would the complainant still be available? In that unlikely event, chances that the information could help Jackson hung closer to none than slim. Still, I had to take a cursory look.

The county clerk's office was on the main floor in the west wing. I had an assistant clerk run the computer index for Griffo's name among plaintiffs and defendants. I wasn't surprised when nothing turned up. The system had been installed over the last six or seven years. That meant I would have to go through the index books, cumbersome old volumes in which all the entries were made by hand.

All of the old records were stored in the sub-basement. I made my way down there and signed the registration book. The room was a kind of gloomy warehouse with aisles stacked high with old records and fussy clerks going back and forth like chipmunks. I picked the two-year period before Griffo's death and tried not to fall asleep as I sat at a long metal table going through book after book. There were plenty of Griffos, but no John. After two hours, I was ready to give up.

I had learned one important lesson about looking at records. The volume you don't check invariably will be the one you'll regret

93

not checking. The entry with Griffo's name was in the last musty red volume the clerk dropped on the table. But it wasn't a brutality complaint. Two months before his death, he had been named as the defendant in a dissolution of marriage petition filed in behalf of Anna C. Griffo.

I jotted down the case number and returned the books. The actual records would be on microfilm. The clerk had to track down the roll and set up the reader. Ten minutes later, I was examining yellowed documents in which Mrs Griffo had sued her husband for divorce on the grounds of irretrievable breakdown. No details were provided. There were no other pleadings, because the petition had been voluntarily withdrawn a month later. Griffo, in fact, didn't even bother to have an attorney file an appearance. A lawyer named Terry Moss represented his wife. I knew Moss slightly. He had since joined the prosecutor's office, where he prosecuted people with an airy sense of self-righteousness.

Emerging into the sultry afternoon from three bleary hours of looking at names and numbers, I went across the street to the City Market and picked up coffee to go. I had left my car parked at a meter down the block. As I crossed the street, I saw an empty space in place of my Toyota.

I cursed under my breath. I'd parked in a tow-in zone and forgot they started towing at three o'clock. That meant I had to walk back to the City-County Building, pay the parking fine, walk six blocks south to the police storage garage, and pay for the tow-in and storage. That meant close to a hundred dollars flew out of my pocket in less than an hour.

I was not in a cheerful mood as I drove north through the rush-hour traffic. I was not happy with our guardians of justice. The last thing I wanted to see was a police cruiser parked in front of my office.

It wasn't a squad car. It was one of the big unmarked maroon Chevrolets the brass and detectives drove. It was blocking one lane of the one-way boulevard with its engine running. The bulky shape inside belonged to Captain Milton O'Hara.

He rolled down the passenger side window. 'Get in, Ritter.'

I got in. There was just enough room to make my legs comfortable under the dashboard computer and the array of radios.

O'Hara turned down the volume and turned up the air conditioning. It was already cold, but he didn't seem to notice. Behind the wheel he looked fatter than I remembered. Mirror sunglasses shielded his eyes.

'You don't look any worse for wear from the other night,' he said. 'Let me pay you a compliment. Not every lawyer I know would have gone into that house. It took some stuff.'

'Thanks. And thanks for not telling me there was a corpse inside. I might have got carried away and tried to make a citizen's arrest. I'm sure you've been waiting out here part of the afternoon to pay me a compliment. I know the department has a grapevine. I didn't know it worked on hyper-speed. Why you?'

O'Hara rubbed his granite jaw with fat knuckles. 'Griffo worked for me. I was a major back then. If I hadn't been on vacation, I might have been there. Who knows, maybe things would have turned out different. Back then you went in on guts. Today we have a whole manual on making safe entry. You can say Johnny saved lives by giving his.'

'I'm sure that's true.'

'Johnny was a good cop. He's got two nephews on the department.'

'Fine officers, no doubt.'

'Only one reason why you'd want Johnny's personnel file. You're working for Jackson.'

'I'm working in behalf of the Jackson family.'

O'Hara raised his gravelly voice a notch.

'And doing what? Trying to dig up dirt on

Griffo to help out the man who killed him?'

'Captain, I'm an attorney doing my job. I'm retracing the circumstances, that's all. Once Jackson is dead, it'll be too late. I'm sorry if this offends the police department in general or you personally, but I'm doing what I'm supposed to do.'

O'Hara snapped off the sunglasses so I could see the contempt burning in his eyes.

'You got something against police officers? Maybe because of what happened to you a couple of years ago?'

He wanted me to throw gasoline on his fire. I kept my voice calm, reasonable, professional.

'No, I don't. Let me tell you something. My uncle was a cop up in Michigan. Worked part-time and mowed lawns on weekends to help raise his family, five kids. He was a damned good cop. And one time he told me something. I remember his exact words. He said, 'Sonny, there are four kinds of police officers. There are good ones, average ones, mediocre ones, and bad ones. In other words, police officers reflect society as a whole. And that ought to scare the hell out of you.''

O'Hara didn't like the message. This time his voice had a bark.

'You don't have to dredge up the mistakes of the past to save a goddamned killer. You don't have to drag Griffo through the mud. Johnny wasn't a perfect cop, but he was a good cop. Why don't you let it be at that?'

O'Hara was beginning to irritate me. I thought he wanted to deliver a message. Now I realized he wanted to intimidate me.

'Look,' I said, 'why get all worked up? The record isn't going to change. Jackson's as good as dead. In a few days he *will* be dead. I don't know what Griffo's sins were, and I'm not interested in hanging them out on the laundry line. But I do have to run the traps, because that's how our system of justice works. Is that so difficult to understand?'

The veins in O'Hara's neck bulged.

'Jackson shot him in cold blood. That fact is undeniable, and it's been undeniable for eight years. For eight years his family and friends have been waiting for justice. For Jackson to pay the penalty. *That's* how our system works. It doesn't need to be screwed up or thrown off the tracks because some smart-ass liberal lawyer thinks maybe he can crucify a dead man.'

I couldn't keep the temper from my voice.

'That's bullshit, O'Hara. I happen to be working with and for a former deputy prosecutor who's about as liberal as you are.'

O'Hara sniffed. He wasn't interested in logic or reality. He was interested in

98

defending and preserving the invisible but very real blue fence protecting the sacred ground where cops congregate in the certainty that no outsider can really understand them.

'You'd better think about what I said,' he warned.

I opened the door and climbed out.

'Thanks for stopping by, captain. Let me leave you with a little law school Latin. *Vescere bracis meis*. It means eat my shorts.'

I slammed the door.

11

Memory is the brain's trickster. It preserves details from experiences that happened in the long-ago past and refuses to let us remember what we had for breakfast two days ago. It erases important events from our minds yet retains a seemingly limitless storehouse of trivia. Memory will laugh at us when we're desperately searching for a piece of information and then spit out the information when we least expect it.

In the middle of the night I awoke out of a sound sleep seeing Johnny Griffo's name typed in fat capital letters on paper bearing the insignia of the Federal Bureau of Investigation.

The window air conditioner was clanking. The alarm clock registered eight minutes after four in red numerals. I splashed cold water on my face, threw on khakis, T-shirt, and running shoes, and went out in the dark.

The night-calling insects had retreated into silence and the early birds were not yet stirring. Along with pockets of mist, stillness hung over the neighborhood, except for the occasional chigger of a lawn sprinkler and the plopping sound of plastic-wrapped newspapers being dropped on driveways. I got coffee to go at the Village Pantry three blocks away and drove to my office.

Phil Curry's file amounted to four thick folders stuck in the bottom of a storage cabinet. With only the desk lamp as illumination I sipped black coffee and leafed through the papers. The first folder contained drafts and copies of our lawsuit, photocopies of federal statutes and court rulings, and a thick swatch of yellow sheets bearing my notes. The second had all the other pleadings, for and against, and rough copies and final versions of our interrogatories. Folder three contained a copy of Curry's personnel file, a censored version of the internal investigation the government conducted based on Phil's complaints, and a half-dozen FBI memos cunningly designed to discredit and destroy him.

Griffo's name came up six times in the fourth folder.

Here were several dozen internal FBI memos Curry had copied and turned over to me as evidence of why the bureau turned on him. Here were reports from confidential informants outlining a system of payoffs running through the police department into the upper reaches of city government. Here

101

were the names of politicians, judges, lawyers, and cops who had taken bribes to look the other way or protect certain people. Here were details of how people who were supposed to uphold the law shielded those who broke it.

The bureau's fussy style required names to be capitalized, and I wasn't surprised to see EARL 'BUTCH' TUNNEY a dozen times or more. With the name came an image: a small, grayish ferret of a man with a flat-top haircut and emotionless shark's eyes. I had seen Tunney around the courts when I was babystepping as a public defender and he was still a licensed bail bondsman. It took time before I learned Butch ran a criminal enterprise stretching across three states. Tunney was the criminal version of the Renaissance man: nightclub owner, used car salesman, con man, fence, gambler, and fixer *extraordinaire*. He was also rumored to be behind a half-dozen murders.

According to the FBI's informants, Sergeant John Griffo went on Tunney's payroll the very week Griffo started his assignment as the late-shift district sergeant in the east side neighborhood featuring a nightclub called the Merry-Go-Round. Although his name wasn't on the liquor license, Tunney owned the place and operated most of his illegal businesses out of a back office. The informants said Griffo made sure no one noticed the hookers, the after-hours drinking, and the frequent arrival in the back alley of trucks without license plates and men with faces you could find in post office lobbies.

Griffo from time to time would let Tunney know whenever someone at headquarters or the prosecutor's office expressed mild interest in Butch's activities. If by chance Tunney's name happened to surface in, say, a murder investigation, Griffo knew how to make the detectives suffer lapses of interest and memory. For this friendly cooperation Griffo received envelopes every month when the assignment slate changed, a new car every year, and generous discounts on certain jewelry that would make its way from other states to the back door of the Merry-Go-Round.

I read the parts on Griffo three times. I counted the eight times the memos mentioned RICHARD 'DICKIE' BUCKLEY, Griffo's partner. I scanned all the other memos and studied four or five of them in detail. Slowly the memory trickster let me recall some of the information from when I had first read it four years ago.

I remembered what I thought the first time I debriefed Curry: here was a man with integrity and guts. What I didn't know then was that the ordeal by fire Phil had been subjected to for going through channels already had begun to affect his mental gyroscope. By the time I realized Phil had one leg down the funhouse slide, the government was suffocating us with red tape, stonewalls, and federal judges unwilling to stick their necks out. Phil, goddamn it, should have been given a medal. Instead the bureaucracy shoved him over the edge and waited until he crashed at the bottom.

So Griffo was a dirty cop. What did that have to do with Jeremiah Jackson? Every wild scenario I could think of collapsed under the weight of logic. Griffo had been dead about four years by the time the FBI logged this information.

Dawn was just breaking when I called Kit. I expected to get her recorder. I got the real thing.

'I know it's you,' she said, sounding wide awake. 'You're calling this early because you have proof Jackson's innocent. In the nick of time.'

'I'm calling this early because I have proof Griffo wasn't so innocent. What are you doing up and about?'

'Are you kidding, Sonny? I've been at the computer for two hours. Thank god, everything's done. But I'm already getting signals from Washington. The Supreme Court's going to turn us down today.'

'Nothing more than you expected, right?'

'Sure, but, you know, I was hoping against hope they'd at least give us a hearing. What's this about Griffo?'

I balanced the memos on my knees. 'FBI stuff Phil Curry gave me several years ago. It makes a pretty good case that Griffo was getting paid off by Butch Tunney. I know, I know. You're going to say, 'So what?''

'You should be a telephone psychic. So what?'

'So nothing, except I think you'd better read this stuff. And keep it under lock and key for me. Can I drop it off?'

'If you make it late. After four, say. I'll make time for you. You can read the final draft of the clemency petition. It's too long. It reads like *War and Peace*.'

'Yeah, well, just don't call it *Crime and Punishment*.'

The dentist's receptionist was arriving as I closed the office. I drove home, shaved, and brushed my teeth. I put on my jogging outfit and headed back into the morning heat.

It was already warm but clouds foaming out of the west kept my body from sizzling. The smell of distant rain was in the air. I headed north up the boulevard.

Running provided exercise but not inspiration. If Griffo happened to be less than honest, the information probably was useless. Maybe he had changed his ways before his fatal encounter with Jackson. According to the memos, Griffo stayed on Tunney's payroll after he transferred to the detective division. Although the informants knew enough details to bolster the accuracy of their information, they were unreliable in one respect. They didn't provide specific dates.

Yet it seemed probable if not certain that Griffo continued doing favors even when he came to work for Captain Milton O'Hara. If so, was O'Hara one of the players? I had scanned the capitalized names in the expectation of finding his, and didn't. Maybe he was just too far in the background for the FBI's snitches to know about.

My shoes pounded on the pebbles along the edge of the boulevard. An occasional car glided past in either direction, invariably exceeding the forty-mile-an-hour limit. I could see the heat rising from the pavement as I left the bridge and the trees began to thin out.

Far off to my left were the movements of walkers and joggers on the Morton Trail. After a long curve I would cross over to run facing any traffic. On the left was a new complex of cookie-cutter apartments in pastel colors, then increasingly smaller lots dotted with trees as the land narrowed towards the river. On the right, a scenic pond fronted another, more expensive apartment development, and after that came a dozen residences with large front yards and mostly one-story ranch-style homes.

A motorcycle can move so fast it's going past by the time you turn in response to the first approaching sound. I heard the cycle coming up from Broad Ripple, and paid no attention. Suddenly it was right behind me.

It's unnerving how loud a big Harley-Davidson sounds when it's next to you. This was more than unnerving — the unexpected, blink-of-an-eye sight of the howling machine coming right at me. As the driver roared up he swerved to come off the pavement on to the berm, and, in a blur, screamed past only inches from my body.

It happened so suddenly I must have jumped high enough to touch a power line. The cycle's wheels had kicked up stones and dust. All I could do was shake my fist at chrome and black leather fading north at high speed. Shaking in relief and disbelief, I stopped and looked around. The son of a bitch had left the road deliberately, to brush dangerously close to me.

Probably still drunk from last night, I decided. I was a quarter-mile away from a popular saloon where bikers congregated. They all looked like pirates in leather, but most of them were perfectly normal middle-class people who sang in church choirs and owned fluffy little dogs.

I crossed the road to run facing the southbound traffic. It would be another half-hour before the volume picked up with drivers heading to work in both directions. I had covered no more than a hundred yards when I heard the faint throb of a motorcycle engine behind me. I kept running, but turned to look.

A black speck came around the bend at high speed. The black speck happened to be a motorcyclist in a black leather jacket, wearing a black and silver helmet and dark sunglasses. The motorcycle had the police department's insignia.

In the nanosecond it took for this information to register in my brain, my body tried to react, and couldn't. Going at least sixty miles an hour, the cycle swerved across the center stripe and headed right at me, like a chrome missile launched from an invisible ship.

I froze.

I wanted to jump out of the way but my legs wouldn't work. I felt my mouth open to yell something, and no words came out. Panic stopped me from doing anything as this roaring menace shot at me and then by me in a cloud of smoke and dust.

I stopped and felt my heart pounding as the cycle and its powerful sound faded into the distance. The gears in my brain were slipping on the oil of fear, but one thought managed to impose itself. *Get the hell out of here.*

I turned south, staying on the west side of the road. When I heard the distant throb of another motorcycle engine coming from around the bend in the direction I was going, I felt helpless and vulnerable. I realized there was no way to run for cover. A stand of pine trees was too thin to provide shelter, and could end up as a trap. It would take at least a full minute to reach an apartment complex down the street, and I didn't have a full minute.

Another cycle, also moving at high speed, was racing south, at my back. The two cycles looked like they might converge. I had maybe three or four seconds to do something other than toss my cookies.

I did the only thing I could think of. I hunched down on the ground and covered my head with my arms.

The noise of the two cycles passing inches away from me in opposite directions was like a roar straight out of hell. A cloud of stones and pebbles pelted me, and dust and dirt clogged my eyes and mouth. But I was unharmed, and the Harleys were fading in both directions, probably to circle around for another pass.

I turned and ran north as fast as I could. Up ahead was a band of trees flanking a gully that ran towards the river bank. With my heart pounding harder I sprinted into the shade and scrambled down into the gully. It went down about ten feet, deep enough to give me time to stumble for eighty yards or so and reach an iron bridge carrying the Morton Trail over the water.

Motorcycles couldn't come down here. And on the trail maybe someone would have a cell phone. Exactly who I might call for help wasn't clear.

Gasping for air and bathed in sweat, I made my way up to the bridge. When I popped my head up, I saw nothing menacing. I climbed over the railing and wiped my eyes with my arms. A dozen people were visible, walkers and runners going north and south.

I began walking at a steady pace. Off to my left I could see the boulevard. I didn't like the view.

Four motorcycles, each with a cop in black leather, moved in unison south along the boulevard, paralleling my progress. I wasn't sure what they planned to do next. I knew I didn't want to know.

Two women in shorts and halters were walking at a leisurely pace in front of me. I closed the distance and walked a few feet behind them. Close up, they were larger than large, like linebackers for the Indianapolis Colts.

One turned her head and said, 'Good morning for a walk, isn't it?'

'Sure is,' I said. 'Until it gets hot.'

'You have to drink plenty of fluids in this weather.'

'You sure do.'

'Look at those motorcycle policemen,' the other woman said. 'How they can wear leather in this heat I'll never know.'

'They must be on their way to a funeral or something,' her friend said.

'Dedicated public servants,' I said, and received nods of agreement.

A few minutes later, trees and buildings blocked the view.

I followed the women into Broad Ripple. By the time the boulevard came back into view, the cycles had moved on.

I took a shortcut to my house and locked the door. After I showered and shaved I peeked through the window blinds. The street was peaceful. The only menace was the grumble of thunder from a rain squall moving in from the west.

Message received and understood.

12

I put on my midnight blue Armani suit with the subtle red stripes, my only white silk shirt, a red and gray striped tie, and black Italian leather shoes. It was my best lawyer's uniform. It told everyone I was part of the power and majesty of the courts. It told motorcycle cops who wanted to play chicken to keep their distance.

On the phone, the day editor at the Indianapolis *Chronicle* told me Bradley Gray would be working on the copy desk all morning. Although Gray's coverage of Jackson's trial included nothing I didn't already know, I wanted to ask him if he had omitted anything important.

I grabbed a handful of last Sunday's paper and stuck the FBI memos inside the comics section. I left the papers with some old plastic coffee cups on the back seat of my car and drove downtown. The speed limit was thirty-five. I drove thirty. Nothing happened except two bursts of rain followed by sun and steam.

Once upon a time the *Chronicle* was a pretty good newspaper. Then a chain bought it up and took out some of the heart and guts and tried to mask the change with color and graphics. I still read the paper religiously because I love to hate the editorials, especially the right-wing screeds written in a prose style similar to *Mein Kampf*. Local news coverage was spotty, although somehow the *Chronicle* had managed to chronicle my arrest and suspension. The news of my reinstatement was deemed not to be news. In the old days the editors would have made sure both were mentioned.

I got a pass from the security guard in the lobby and directions from the receptionist at the second-floor newsroom. I had given Gray a few tips on stories in my public defender days. The Brad Gray sitting alone behind a computer at a horseshoe-shaped desk was hard to recognize. He was so fat, he looked like two Brad Grays.

'Excuse me,' I said. 'I'm Sonny Ritter. Can I talk to you for a couple of minutes?'

Gray appeared to be glad to have company. He removed his spectacles and rubbed his eyes. He had a round face, graying brown hair, and a spade-shaped salt-and-pepper beard.

'Well, haven't seen you in a coon's age. Pull up a chair. I'm not doing anything important. What brings you around here?'

'Jeremiah Jackson. I'm working on the appeal.'

Gray's short burst of laughter conveyed surprise and skepticism.

'There's a name I haven't heard in awhile. Strange to think that trial was, what? Nine or ten years ago? Jeremiah Jackson. You say that name and I think of Jerusalem Sterne. Helluva man, old Jerusalem.'

'He was kind of a legend around here, wasn't he?'

Gray's ample body shook and what might have been mirthful nostalgia shone in his eyes. All around us, telephones rang and teletypes chattered, but only a dozen or so reporters and editors were working, all of them tapping on computer keyboards while talking on telephones.

'Old Jerusalem,' Gray said. 'One thing about that trial, he was sober the whole time. Imagine he got bombed right after, then he died. Old Jerusalem. Man, was he crafty. And drink? Like a whale, not a fish. Tell you a story. Sterne was giving a summation to a jury once when a half-pint of rye fell out of his jacket. Without missing a beat, he bent over and picked it up and said, 'Sorry, your honor. Evidence in another case.' And went on with his summation.'

Gray chuckled wetly. 'Anyway, if you're

here to ask about misconduct or suppressed evidence or anything like that, I can't help you. Jackson didn't have a chance. You knew he was guilty if you saw the videotape. Getting the needle pretty soon, isn't he?'

'It looks like it.'

Gray rubbed his backside and readjusted his bulk on the chair.

'Well, lethal injection isn't so bad. Tell you, I covered an execution once. God, decades ago. Killer went to the chair. One was enough for me, thanks.'

'So there's nothing you can tell me about the trial, the evidence, the circumstances, rumors, whispers, anything that didn't make your stories.'

'Can't think of a thing. Sorry. Pretty much went by the book, as I recall. No sympathy for a cop killer.'

'Justice?'

'I think so.' Gray pursed his lips. 'I'm surprised he used up all his appeals so soon. Or I guess he hasn't. I've been on the copy desk for five years, you know. Those kids covering the courthouse, they don't know how to unpin their diapers. I'd help you if I could. And I can't think of anyone who can.' He rubbed his forehead with his fingers. 'Well, wait a minute. That's not entirely true. You know who Leland Hurt is?'

'Sure. Reporter here, isn't he?'

'Retired. A legend, like Sterne was. Best investigative reporter this town's ever seen. And I remember something odd. I remember Lee laughing and telling me the jury got it wrong. The Jackson jury. Wouldn't explain. Memory's funny, isn't it? I just remembered that out of the blue.'

'Hurt thought the jury was wrong but wouldn't say why? The implication being he knew something they didn't know?'

'Hell if I know,' Gray said in a tone of indifference. 'You'll have to ask him. Star Liquors, in Broad Ripple. He works there part-time. Should be there now.'

'I know the place. It used to be my home away from home. Listen, can you do me a small favor? I'd like to get the old clips on Griffo. You can get them without any hassle. Send them to my home.'

'I don't mind, but, I'll tell you, some of these new librarians, they don't know how to find their armpits. They'll have to go back on microfilm.'

'I appreciate your help.'

I had an unpleasant mission before I could look up Leland Hurt. I had to pay my respects at the calling for Phil Curry. I had to put in an appearance at the funeral home because I was the last person to talk to him.

That the mortuary was only three blocks from Star Liquors made it easier.

The ride north was as uneventful as the ride south. It had turned sunny, warm but not yet unbearably humid. A dozen or so cars were parked in the lot at the funeral home. Inside, the place had the sweet smell of perfumed death.

A mortician dressed like a man ready to chaperone at the prom directed me to the parlor. It was a spacious, wallpapered room with a closed casket, three flower displays, an unoccupied kneeling bench, and two dozen chairs for visitors. There were no visitors, only a gaunt woman in black I recognized as Curry's sister.

I stood in front of the coffin for a moment. I whispered a prayer and remembered all the good things about Phil. He deserved a better fate, a better legacy.

'Sonny Ritter,' I reminded the woman. 'We met a long time ago. I'm sorry, so very sorry.'

Her thin face was as blank as cardboard. She didn't look at all like her brother. She had a rosary twisted between her fingers.

'Thank you.' Her voice barely squeezed the two words out.

'Phil was worried about the kids.'

'Yes, they're fine, all things considered. My

husband's watching them today. Everything will be fine.'

'Good, good. He was counting on you. I wish I . . . '

Her eyes suddenly flared, burning at me.

'You were there. You talked to him. Can you explain . . . it?'

'I'm not sure anyone can explain what brings a man to that point. I'm not sure anybody could help him. Everything that happened he planned that way, more or less.'

Pain thickened her voice. 'But to be . . . *shattered* . . . by so many bullets. How horrible. How could he?'

'I really don't know the answer. Suicide just isn't as easy for some people as it is for others. I don't pretend to understand why.' I touched her shoulder. 'I don't mean to be gruesome, but it was sort of like stepping in front of a firing squad. Death was instantaneous.'

A sob shook her upper body. 'I know you're right. I'm so sorry. So sorry.'

I stood there for a long minute sharing her confusion and suffering.

'I'm sorry more people aren't here,' I said.

'Well, it's early, isn't it?'

'Take care of yourself.'

'Thank you. You, too.'

I felt like the air in the parlor couldn't be

breathed any longer. I was glad to get outside.

A few minutes later, I walked into the air-conditioned liquor store. For the first time, I realized the silver-haired man who worked behind the counter once had been the state's greatest investigative reporter.

'Afternoon,' he said. 'What can we get for you?'

'I'm Sonny Ritter, attorney. I'd like to talk to you, Mr Hurt.'

'Really? You're one of our regulars. Or used to be. You want to talk to me?'

There was something distinguished about the man, perhaps the way he kept his shirt buttoned and his sleeves down, often with cufflinks. Maybe it was the fullness of his silver hair or the thick white moustache which reminded me of my father's, full and clipped and somewhat formal. Hurt was probably in his early or mid-seventies. He had a deep voice, a voice accustomed to conveying authority.

He had been working crossword puzzles in a small book. He removed his reading glasses, capped his pen, and stood behind the counter, his deep brown eyes conveying wary curiosity.

'I'm helping on an appeal for a man named Jeremiah Jackson,' I said. 'He killed a cop eight years ago and he's about to be executed.

I was talking to Brad Gray down at the paper, and he said you told him once that Jackson shouldn't have been convicted.'

Hurt snorted. 'Gray said that? Must be getting soft in the head. Sorry, I can't help you.'

'If there's anything you can remember, even an iota of information, it might save a man's life.'

Hurt snorted again. 'Why should I give a tinker's dam about a man's life? I'm out of that stuff now. I'm not a player. I have my scrapbook and my jazz records, and I work here a few hours to earn a few bucks. You want to know why? You should see the *Chronicle* pensions. Pitiful. Peanuts. No, I can't help you.'

'Can't or won't?'

Hurt studied me. From his breast pocket he removed a brown leather case and gently tucked the glasses inside.

'Ritter, did you say? Mr Ritter, let me tell you a little bit about history. When the crusaders took Jerusalem in 1099, they slaughtered approximately seventy-thousand inhabitants. Men, women, and children. Butchered them, then gave thanks to God. Seventy thousand people. Dead, like that. Now, do you know what happened in August of 1931?'

'No, sir, I don't.'

'Great floods struck China. It's estimated that three million, seven hundred thousand people perished. Think of it. Nearly four million people drowned like rats in a matter of hours. Men, women, children. It's beyond your imagination.'

'Your point being . . . '

Hurt raised his eyebrows. 'Do you think it matters a smidgen if Jackson dies? It doesn't. It certainly doesn't matter to me. How many thousands of people have died while we've been talking? I told you, I'm not a player. So, save your breath, and good luck to you.'

'You used to be a player, Mr Hurt. You used to be a helluva player. I'm betting there was a time when you had a white charger saddled up whenever you sensed an injustice. If there's an injustice here, forget the importance of Jackson and think of the importance of good people doing the right thing.'

I hoped this little speech would stir the embers of yesteryear. Instead Hurt looked at me like I had started speaking in tongues.

'Fellow, let me tell you something. That time did exist. I galloped that charger more times than you could count. Tilted at more windmills than anybody else. Got sued a dozen times. Had lawyers like you trying to peel the skin off my rectum with hot tongs. Hell, back about the time you were being potty-trained, I was arrested on a frame-up. Arrested because some powerful people wanted to silence the newspaper. Did my bit for God and country.'

He raised his hands as if to shove his point home.

'And you know what? When someone else bought the paper, some out-of-state corporation interested in the color of ink on the bottom line, I no longer mattered. Got put out to pasture. That's it. I stopped caring. Try to understand that, all right?'

'Try to understand my position.'

'You know something? Each year the paper gives an in-house award in my name for investigative reporting. Know how much the winner gets? Two hundred and fifty dollars.' If laughter can be sad, his was sad. 'That's what my kind of reporting is worth.'

'So you're telling me I'm just wasting my time?'

'No, I didn't say that.'

'Then what are you saying?'

'I'm not saying anything. You're a grown-up man with a law degree. You make your own decisions.'

'If you were me, what would you do?'

'Keep digging. You never know what you'll turn up.'

'Keep digging where? For what?'

Hurt shrugged his shoulders with the indifference of a bitter old warrior too tired to pick up his axe or shield.

A bell rang on the front door, signaling the arrival of a customer and the end of our interview.

13

When your clients include Penrod Pharmaceuticals, the world's third- or fourth-largest
drug company, you don't have to get your
decorating ideas at Wal-Mart. Stepping off
the elevator into the reception area of Ritter
Ritter Talmadge & Stokely was like arriving at
the Vatican.

Rich oak paneling covered the walls. The
ceilings were edged with fruit-and-leaf patterns. The wine-red carpet was two inches
thick. The portraits of the founders and
partners had expensive frames and tiny
electric beacons. As clients wondered whether
to genuflect, they would get the warm feeling
that their money would be going to a higher
cause.

I sank into a leather chair and waited while
the receptionist located Kit. I hoped Meg
would wander by. Instead a door opened and
a group of men emerged, muttering like
cardinals who had just visited the pope. All of
them had silver hair and expensive suits. They
began walking in different directions. One of
them walked right up to me.

Carson Talmadge Ritter, Jr, prided himself

on his wardrobe. He favored double-breasted, padded-shoulder tweeds tailored in London. With his ruddy thin face, shock of silver-gray hair, snowy sprigs of eyebrow, and sharply clipped moustache, my father looked like a British diplomat worrying about the future of the empire. He was acutely aware of the effect this had on clients and their checkbooks. Once, I remembered, he made a rare joke to my mother. He said he raised his fee every time he found a new gray hair.

In his soft slate-blue eyes I thought I glimpsed a familiar flash, a perplexing expression wondering how his apple had fallen so far from the tree. Our handshake and stiff embrace captured something of our differences. What might take a book to explain could be summarized in a line. He would represent Thomas Jefferson; I would represent Jefferson's slave mistress, Sally Hemings.

'Dad.'

'Sonny, you look . . . good. Working with Kit must agree with you.'

'It does, Dad. She's a heckuva lawyer.'

'Yes, indeed. We haven't seen you since Easter, Sonny. You might call your mother.'

His eyes reminded me that mother never would recover fully from the shock and shame of seeing her only begotten son arrested and suspended.

'I will, sir. I've been very busy. Building up the practice.'

My father's lips tightened the way they always did when he was pinching a thought off his tongue.

'This Jackson thing. Too bad. You two've done your best.'

'The ballgame isn't over yet, Dad. We've still got an out or two.'

'Yes, well. Take care of yourself, Sonny. Call your mother. Stop by when you can.'

He had noticed Kit at the end of the hallway, and his perfunctory hug terminated our reunion. Kit wore a blue-and-white polka-dot skirt with an over-sized collar, a white bolero jacket, and glossy white patent leather heels. She signaled me to follow into her office.

'Nice to see you two together,' she said. 'I can tell he hasn't been happy not seeing you.'

'I have lovely parents who would like nothing better to spend an entire day iterating and reiterating where I went wrong.'

Kit's office was about the size of the tennis court behind the home where I grew up. She had a desk big enough to hold a pickup truck, the latest computer gadgets, designer chairs you could fall asleep in, and a conference area about the size of my entire office. What always got me, though, was the fireplace. Thirty-five stories up in the air, and a fake fireplace of Italian marble.

The way files and folders were scattered everywhere suggested she had more clients than she could handle. But then she had access to a pool of interns and secretaries.

'You'll be surprised at who you find in the funny pages these days,' I said as I dropped the comics on her desk.

'Who?' Kit kicked off her heels and made herself comfortable in her leather ladder-back chair.

'A certain canonized police officer, for one. Plus a few other saints from the city government.'

Kit dug out the memos and put on her reading glasses as she sat behind her desk. 'You can read my clemency petition while I read this.'

I took a chair near the window. Beyond the glass the city offered an inspiring view. The sun glinted off the dome of the state capitol. The statues of Civil War heroes could be seen on the monument in the heart of downtown. Glossy new buildings rose where dusty ones once stood. From high above everything looked orderly, safe, and clean. Like a fireplace in the sky, it was a wonderful illusion.

Kit's petition was concise and powerful without being emotional. She cited every precedent worth citing. She enunciated every moral argument worth arguing. It was such a strong pleading, I knew she would want to save it for a case where it might do some good.

'Good stuff,' I remarked to break the silence.

'Thanks. These memos . . . Sonny, this is *dynamite*.'

'Dynamite without a blasting cap, maybe.'

Shaking her luxuriant blonde hair, she took off her glasses and stared at me.

'Judge Ramsey, that hypocrite. And old Judge Crocker, him I would have guessed. The mayor's chief fundraiser. The deputy chief of police. Do you realize what you have here?'

'Yeah. To quote Bill Shakespeare, words, words, words.'

Kit resumed reading. For the next ten minutes neither of us said anything. At one point she cursed under her breath, and a few minutes later she actually snorted in contempt. Then she dropped the memos on her desk and looked at me with an expression of perplexity.

'I don't know what to say. It certainly doesn't paint a pretty picture. It's hard to believe there were two wide-open brothels protected by the police. And collecting campaign contributions from gamblers, it's disturbing.'

'Gamblers, bootleggers, and drug dealers. Plus kickbacks from anyone who wanted a city contract.'

'I'm shocked nothing was done with this. If I had this when I was with the prosecutor's office, we would have had a grand jury running day and night.'

'Only if your boss gave the okay. I'm not so sure he would. Anyway, that's the past.'

'Why didn't the FBI do anything?'

I heard Curry's voice in my head as I answered.

'Phil Curry was a straight-arrow brick agent who did background investigations and routine fraud cases. Then he got assigned to the organized crime squad. Pretty soon he started running across memos like these, and it occurred to him the bureau had a lot of information about corruption and hadn't done diddly squat with it.'

'Why not?'

'Lots of reasons. The local office was one of the worst in the country. The agent in charge was a boozer. Some of the agents were overly friendly with the city cops. Here's the kicker, though. The agents were rated according to

130

their ability to develop informants. The more informants and the more paperwork, the bigger the bonus, and it kept Washington happy. So they could log all of this information, get credit for it, and never open investigations.'

'Incredible.'

'But true, oh, so true. Anyway, Curry wanted to run with this stuff. When some of the other agents began noticing, they started trying to squelch him. Well, Phil was a hard-head. The more they squelched, the harder he went. Pretty soon he was getting threatened, pushed around, reassigned, the whole nine yards. He was ordered to take a psychological test. His gun was stolen. Files disappeared. He was charged with all kinds of infractions. In short, they were out to get him, they mainly being three other agents. He had to get out. That's where I came in.'

'Why didn't you use these memos?'

'Planned to. We were going to drop a bomb on this town. I was going to file the memos as exhibits. When the government found out, well, that was the beginning of the end. For our lawsuit, and for Curry as well. The feds just flat-out circled the wagons, including the U.S. attorney, who was mortified because he hadn't done shit about any of this and some of these people were members of his club.

There wasn't a judge in the circuit with the guts to go against the entire federal establishment in behalf of an exagent who was starting to unravel from months of unbelievable tension and pressure. End of crusade.'

'I remember how upset you were.'

'I felt sad, Kit, because Curry deserved better. Realistically, though, he wasn't quite the great witness he might have been earlier. Anyway, we struck out. Then I had my own little problem. You know the rest. To tell you the truth, I'd forgotten about most of these allegations.'

Kit began rereading parts of the memos.

'Sonny, I know this is going to sound strange, but are you sure the way Curry died is what you think it was?'

I had thought the same thing myself.

'Did the cops kill Curry because he had information about corruption? Uh-uh. The stuff's been stored away for ages. The police didn't push Phil to the breaking point. They didn't get him fired and cause him to shoot his wife. Besides, I saw the gun he stuck in the back of his collar.'

'It is ironic, though, isn't it?'

'Ironic and sad. But it's important in relation to Griffo, not to Curry.'

Kit looked puzzled. 'How? I don't see what

132

bearing this could have for us.'

'It tells me Griffo wasn't the saint he was painted to be. That bothers me. I don't like surprises. I don't like discovering a man was something so drastically different than what everybody was led to believe. Because if one thing was so different, maybe something else will be different, too.'

'Give me a for-instance.'

'Don't have any. But I'm anxious to watch the videotape in slow-motion.'

'How about if we watch it at your place tonight? I'll bring supper, around seven.'

'You bring the steaks. I'll supply the Scotch.'

'In the meantime,' Kit said, 'I'm making my pitch to the parole board in the morning. What about you?'

'I still haven't looked at Sterne's files. And I thought I might try to talk to Dickie Buckley.'

'Buckley won't give you the time of the day. You know that.'

'I do know that. I also know Buckley was the closest man to Griffo when he went down. I know I have to face him, because if I don't, I'll always wonder if Buckley might have said something he didn't mean to say.'

I debated whether to tell Kit about the motorcycle menaces, and decided not to.

14

The building where Jerusalem Sterne once labored was a turn-of-the-nineteenth-century flat-iron structure a block and a half from the *Chronicle*. If the bar association wanted young lawyers to know what a law office looked like in the golden-olden days, they could preserve the musty, dusty collection of desks, chairs, and bookshelves in an exhibit. There wasn't a computer in sight, and one old magnificent cherry desk actually had an inkwell.

Miss Quinn, who was old and magnificent herself, acted as a kind of curator. She had been Sterne's secretary for forty years and, for another ten, the secretary of Mr Alden Kellerman, Esq, Sterne's younger partner, who still practiced on a limited basis. Younger meant Kellerman was now seventy-nine. I hoped to talk to him, but Miss Quinn explained he was on a family trip in Canada. However, Mr Kellerman had authorized Miss Quinn to dig out Mr Sterne's old files on the Jackson case for Mr Ritter.

She escorted me to an otherwise bare desk where a foot-tall folder had been deposited.

'Would you like a cup of coffee, Mr Ritter?' She was a tiny silver bird, probably in her late seventies, who had aged, like certain old classic books do, with a kind of fading elegance.

'I would love a cup of coffee.'

A few minutes later, Miss Quinn returned. The cup and saucer were delicate and painted with golden flowers; her hands were wrinkled but graceful; the coffee was black and thick.

'One doesn't forget a man like Mr Jackson,' she said, her voice gentled by years of talking in an office where conversations were mannered and polite. 'He didn't strike me as a killer. But his language . . . '

'I had a strong dose of it. Mr Sterne did a good job for Jackson. He kept him alive for eight years, anyway.'

'Mr Sterne didn't think Mr Jackson committed capital murder. Mr Sterne distrusted witnesses who were too certain of their testimony. He didn't trust people who were overly certain. He didn't believe them.'

'Any one in particular?'

'Not that I can recall. Mr Sterne was very upset when the judge imposed the death penalty. We watched the videotape, you know. It made me quite sad.'

'I wonder what Mr Sterne thought about the tape.'

'Well, I know he believed it was inflammatory and therefore prejudicial. But he said Mr Jackson would have been convicted even without the tape.'

Miss Quinn went back to her desk. Over the next two hours, the phone never rang once.

Most of the material had been duplicated in the trial transcript or appeals records. Among the things I hadn't seen was a thin sheaf of manufacturer's specifications on the weapon confiscated from Jackson. There were photographic reproductions of the same model and other models and illustrations of various accessories available at various prices. The sheets provided detailed information about the mechanics and operation. The automatic model could empty the magazine in less than three seconds; the semi-automatic took a second and a half longer. Either way, the things were fast and lethal. It was interesting if not necessarily useful.

I thumbed through the remaining papers. Sterne's notes were hard to decipher, mostly pencil scribbles with his own special abbreviations. I looked for surprises: telltale letters, phone numbers, mysterious names, or reference to the personnel records, backgrounds, or private habits of Griffo, Buckley, or the other officers on the scene.

I found one. A fading pink telephone message slip, the notations written in ink from a fountain pen, carried a date two weeks before the start of the trial. It asked Mr Sterne to return the call of L. Hurt, *Chronicle*.

Other than the note, the only thing I found interesting was a packet containing six photographs, each eight-by-ten inches, in grainy color. They were autopsy photos, showing different views, including close-ups, of a naked Johnny Griffo. For the first time, I felt sorry for the man. Lying dead on a cold metal table, he looked human in a way the television images failed to convey.

The pictures showed more black than red; that is, the bullet wounds appeared as dark smudges rather than gaping holes revealing muscle or tissue. The holes were smaller than I expected, about the size of cocktail olives. The holes in the chest and legs didn't necessarily stand out; the two in the skull couldn't be missed.

If the photo spread provided a graphic and disturbing reminder that a human being had been brutally cut down, the autopsy report turned him into an abstraction. The language was impersonal and clinical. The coroner's drawing for identifying the bullet entry points looked more like a child's stick figure, completely lacking features.

When I finished, I asked Miss Quinn if there was any chance Mr Sterne had left other notes not in the file. Maybe he kept a journal or diary.

'No, I don't think so,' she said. 'Mr Sterne really didn't take a lot of notes. He was famous for his memory, you know. It was very close to a photographic memory.'

'Perhaps Mr Kellerman helped Mr Sterne in someway.'

'Help Mr Sterne? Mr Kellerman? I don't think so.'

'Then this is your complete record on the Jackson case?'

'What we retained, yes. Most material was discarded upon Mr Sterne's death. This I had to get from the archives.'

'I didn't find in the file one thing I expected to find. Newspaper articles.'

Miss Quinn chuckled, and fairly blushed.

'To tell you the truth, Mr Sterne didn't read the newspapers. Said he had no use for them. He did videotape the TV news shows when he made an appearance. He was quite fascinated by how he looked, as opposed to how he thought he would look. Also by what they showed compared to what they taped. Sound bites, I believe they're called.'

'I noticed a message for Mr Sterne to

contact a reporter named Lee Hurt. Does it ring a bell?'

'No, I'm afraid not.'

'Do you know what happened to the TV tapes? I mean the news shows Mr Sterne taped?'

'Oh, disposed of years ago. Mr Sterne wasn't interested in them after he saw them once. You can use a videotape more than once, you know.'

'Did he have the tape of the shooting analyzed?'

'Why, no, I don't believe so. Mr Sterne was a very shrewd observer. I remember him saying how futile the whole thing was, because everyone was so upset due to the violent death of a police officer. His strategy was to de-emphasize that tape, as if it weren't important. His goal wasn't to have Mr Jackson exonerated, but to avoid the death penalty. As I say, Mr Sterne was quite upset when that, you know, happened. Or at least will happen. In a few days, I believe.'

'Three days, unless the parole board recommends clemency, or at least a delay, which isn't likely.' I handed her the coffee cup. 'Mr Sterne worked around the county courts for many, many years, did he not?'

'Five decades, yes. Oh, the stories he could tell. He was in the state senate, in the 1950s, you know. Hard to believe it's been half a century, isn't it? He had an eye for higher office, but . . . '

'If you're referring to his drinking habits, I know his reputation.'

She seemed embarrassed by the comment, as if an outsider had learned a family secret.

'In the later years, I'm afraid. I can assure you Mr Sterne served his clients vigilantly, even when . . . '

'I'm sure you could tell a few stories yourself, Miss Quinn. The characters who've come through these doors. Tell me, do you recall if Mr Sterne used any particular bail bondsman for his clients?'

Miss Quinn fidgeted with her hands as she pondered the question.

'No, I don't believe so. Barbara Cotton and Bernie Jenner quite a bit. Bernie probably more than anyone, I would think.'

'What about Earl Tunney? Known as Butch Tunney.'

'Not for bonding. Mr Sterne was Mr Tunney's *attorney* on several matters.'

'Do you recall what they were?'

'No. The name, yes. A face, no. There were so many.'

'You wouldn't happen to have records on those cases?'

'No. The files were kept for a certain period

140

and then most of them destroyed. There was no need. I was surprised we still had *these* files.'

'You've been very patient. You make a wonderful cup of coffee.'

'Thank you. With Mr Kellerman on vacation, the phone doesn't ring as much.'

I asked if she would make copies of the autopsy report and photos.

'Mr Kellerman said you can have the file, if you want it. We certainly have no use for it.'

15

Instead of steaks, Kit brought four cartons of Chinese food from a takeout joint. We had a couple of healthy belts of Cutty while I warmed the dinner in the oven. With a look of disgust, Kit kicked off her shoes, knotted a towel on her waist, and began wiping the kitchen table.

'Don't you ever clean this place?'

'Sure. I clean it myself.'

'How often? Once a year?'

'I clean the kitchen every two or three weeks. I eat out a lot. I like eating by myself. I like loneliness. Loneliness is nonfattening.'

The noise of the neighbor mowing his lawn in the early evening came through the window while we ate. Kit leafed through Sterne's papers between bites of food and sips of Scotch or ice water.

'Don't look at the autopsy pictures while you're eating,' I said.

'Why not? I've seen hundreds of autopsy pictures. I watched a couple of autopsies when I was a deputy prosecutor. I left when the coroner took out the saw to cut into the skull. These aren't particularly gory. They look strange, for some reason.'

'Strange in what way?'

'I don't know, just strange. Maybe it's just looking at this man after the things I've heard about him lately.'

'Add this to the ingredients. Griffo was tied in to Tunney. Sterne was Tunney's attorney. Or at least represented him in several criminal matters.'

'I'm not surprised. Sterne represented thousands of people. He must have known Tunney from around the courts. Do you know any particulars?'

'Uh-uh. You have to figure it was a long time ago, long before the shooting.'

'And figure Sterne didn't necessarily know of any connection between Tunney and Griffo. So a coincidence.'

'*Another* coincidence.'

Kit chewed silently for a minute. Then she said, 'I'm the suspicious sort. But, the truth is, Sterne did a good job for Jackson.'

'So it would seem. I don't suppose, just for argument's sake, that Tunney importuned Sterne to make sure certain information never came up, like his relationship with Griffo.'

'That's assuming Sterne wanted to challenge Griffo's character, which he didn't, and assuming there was some way Sterne would have known about the relationship. I don't think so. Sterne knew casting aspersions on Griffo would hurt, not help. We'll never know for sure. Tunney isn't about to walk in and tell all.'

'It's funny about personal relationships, isn't it? From the outside we have no idea what's going on inside. It's like watching a puppet show. We see the puppet but not the hands.'

We ate in silence. It had been a long day for both of us.

'Can I ask you a personal question?' Kit said. 'What really happened between you and Meg?'

'What happened? I got run down by a truck, and it turned out I was the driver.'

'Meaning what?'

'I don't know. I got too wrapped up in things. Too wrapped up in my cases. Curry, for instance. And I was drinking more than I realized. I thought everything was okay at home because Meg never said it wasn't. I was too stupid to ask. By the time I looked, it was too late. Then, as you know, I cleverly managed to screw things up worse. Meg said she didn't know me any more, and maybe she was right.'

'You crawled into your shell and didn't want to talk to anyone. To be honest, I thought there might have been other women.'

'No other women, at least of the flesh. The other woman was the law, if you don't mind the cliché. Since then, she's given me the cold shoulder. Meg, I mean.'

'Your meeting the other day had an effect, I can tell you that. I think she's still got a little thing for you. And you for her?'

I dropped my eyes. 'It's a feeling of helplessness. Like I unwittingly caused an accident and don't know how to undo it. She built a fortress around herself so I couldn't hurt her any more. I just wanted to *talk* to her, and she wouldn't. When I get up in the morning, I call her number, just to listen to her voice on the recorder. Silly, isn't it?'

'Not so silly. You know, you haven't changed that much since law school, except you've created this persona, this attitude about yourself, so people can't get close, so they won't know how sensitive you really are.'

'We all play roles, and sometimes we turn into the character we've been impersonating.'

We had finished the food. I poured more Scotch in both glasses. Velvet darkness had descended upon the neighborhood with a slight break in the humidity.

I saluted Kit with my glass. 'Now it's my turn to ask you a personal question.'

'Shoot.'

'Why'd you take this case? You've never been big on capital punishment one way or the other. You knew this was a loser going in.'

'I suppose because of the way Mrs Jackson looked when she came to the office. Like she was visiting the White House or something. This little old lady with a handful of dollars who looked at me like I was Joan of Arc and I could save her son when nobody else could. I just couldn't say no, even though, practically speaking, I didn't have the time.'

'I wondered about that handful of dollars. I'm not real good on arithmetic, but I think you gave me more money than she gave you. Talk about a persona. Under that beautiful ex-prosecutor's costume beats a soft heart.'

Kit couldn't stop from blushing, and the color brought out her freckles.

'Maybe. The truth is, I had no business taking the case. My dance card was already full. You've been a godsend, really.'

'Even though I've come up with more questions than answers?'

Kit sipped her drink contemplatively, and finally said, 'You asked about capital punishment. I've always supported it because society is damned with certain predators who need to be removed, the Mansons and Bundys. But I was never passionate on the subject. I could live with whatever the Supreme Court decides according to the philosophical drift of the moment. Now I'm not so sure. All this new information may not have an actual bearing on the shooting, but it does raise questions about the parties, questions that might have been pertinent at trial. It's just that, I don't know, I'm not sure J.J. deliberately shot Griffo. If it was unintentional, as he says, then what? An eye for an eye? You tell me. The closer you get to the issue, the more confusing it becomes.'

'It's rare to see you confused. Kit Lake, who's always sure about everything. Or are we getting inside a persona again?'

She replayed my own words.

'We all play roles, and sometimes we turn into the character we've been impersonating. I suppose there's something else. At the firm, you get comfortable and stuffy. Every day you're more comfortable and stuffier. I know they want to develop more of a criminal specialty, but only for their big clients. You have a good effect on me, Sonny. You remind me that there's another world on the street.'

'Well, now that you're telling secrets, answer me this one. Why'd you leave the prosecutor's office? I know it's not money. I know you're interested in public affairs. I always had a kind of feeling you might run for something yourself.'

Kit began picking up the debris on the table and putting it in a plastic disposal bag.

'I wonder if I made a mistake,' she said. 'The fact is, I miss it. No, it's not the money. It's just that I had to try a big private firm, to see if I could make my mark, so to speak. I realize now that the more important you become, the farther away you are from your roots. I think I always had a kind of knack for criminal law. Maybe I watched too many old *Perry Mason* episodes with my parents.'

The phone rang.

When I didn't answer after five rings, Kit said, 'It could be for me.'

I picked up the receiver. 'Sonny Ritter.'

A man's voice, possibly muffled through a hand or handkerchief, said, 'I've got the dirt you want on Griffo. Understand, I'm sticking my neck out. There's a new housing development called Candlewood in Johnson County, on Bronson road, three miles east of Ind. 37. Meet me at ten o'clock sharp. Come alone, and no funny business.'

'How do I know . . . ?'

'You don't know anything. Ten o'clock. I won't wait.'

He hung up.

'Who was that?' Kit asked.

'A mystery man who wants to meet in the

middle of nowhere to supposedly dish out dirt on Griffo.'

'Where's the middle of nowhere?'

'A housing development or something in Johnson County, at ten o'clock, by my lonesome.'

'I'll go with you.'

I laughed. 'Kit, chances are it's Buckley or one of his buddies with a wild-goose chase. I probably won't even go.'

'Yes, you will.'

'Let's watch the tape and then decide.'

We watched the tape. Kit sat on the sofa with the remote control and I sat in the easy chair. The first six minutes, in regular speed, were new. The camera started rolling as the police units assembled around the corner from the house where Jackson and Mason were hiding. There wasn't much talking as the officers put on their vests and checked their weapons. There were three exchanges between the camera operator and his sound man, both speaking in clipped accents. The weather was cool and cloudy. The Brits were hoping to record things naturally, without narration or commentary; that was to be added later.

I recognized Buckley first. He was a sullen, stocky man whose hair was so black and thick it looked like a wig. He was obviously running the show, but not by barking orders. Everyone seemed to know their roles. Serving warrants was a matter of routine. The camera caught Griffo taking several puffs on a cigarette and flicking the butt away with his finger. The cops didn't look concerned or tense, but you could tell from how the camera jumped and jerked that the operator was edgy.

In fact, as they began moving the camera followed unsteadily. A voice — it might have been Buckley's — told the Brits to stay back until he was certain the scene had been secured. It only took a few seconds to go around the corner. A dog barked nearby. Like commandos, the officers fanned out around the house, and Buckley could be seen signaling two men to go around the sides.

Here the speed slowed. The figures of the police moved as if they were walking on flypaper. The camera had moved down the street and been positioned behind a car not quite in front of the house, putting everything at an angle, and then moving to a close-up view. Kit pushed a button to move ahead to the point where Griffo moved from a crouching position at the corner of the house, and, bent downward, went up the concrete steps. The front of the house was gray, like the day. Slowly, the other figures moved closer.

Griffo moved to the door in slow motion. Kit switched to regular speed, we watched the entry and the shooting, and then rewound the tape to watch the same portion in slow motion. Griffo hit the door with his left shoulder, and it went open. He turned, his back to the camera, and went slowly into a shadow. Then he collapsed, face down but his body twisting, and in excruciating slow motion you could see pieces of wood splintering from the door and frame.

We watched the same segment in slow motion again, then the remainder in regular speed.

In regular speed the sound was much better, and the quick double cough of gunshots clearly came from upstairs seconds before Griffo went in. Jackson's gun had an odd sound, like a typewriter carriage popping loudly. Three other officers went in on a burst of gunfire. For a moment, the camera didn't move, as if the device itself, as well as its operator, was shocked at what it had witnessed.

A moment later, the camera jumped and moved up the short front lawn to the steps. It recorded two figures in black and blue kicking a man on the ground. Then everything went black.

As always this mini-movie of a man's

sudden death left me with a sickened feeling.

'You want to watch it again?' Kit asked.

'Not really.'

'See anything new?'

'Not really.'

'Do you want to go meet your mystery man now?'

'Not really.'

16

By the time we crossed the county line, going south along the interstate, a bright moon lightened the night sky and a black cloud darkened my thoughts. I decided Kit should know certain things before she landed with me in a potentially risky situation.

'A police captain came to see me the other day,' I said. 'He suggested looking into Griffo's background wasn't such a good idea.'

'Who was it?'

'Captain O'Hara. Griffo's former boss.'

'Did he threaten you?'

'Not exactly. He just said the police don't like the idea of radical lawyers raising questions about hero cops on behalf of a convicted killer.'

'That's understandable. Is this the same O'Hara who was quoted about the Curry shooting?'

'The very same.'

'The blue wall of silence. I hope you put him in his place. Politely, but firmly.'

'Well, there's more. While I was jogging, a squad of motorcycle cops showed up to give me an escort. We played a fun little game of chicken. I was the chicken.'

'That's not funny. You should have told me. I would have filed a complaint with the chief of police. You weren't hurt, I take it?'

'Except for stripping the gears on my sphincter, no. My point is, Kit, these people seem to have themselves in a dither, and I can't predict what they'll do next.'

'They're officers of the law. They've waited a long time to see the man who killed one of their own executed. Naturally, they're worked up. Under the uniforms, they're human. They're going to bitch and bellow. But that's all they're going to do.'

'Maybe. But people like Butch Tunney do more than bitch and bellow.'

'If Tunney warned you instead of a police captain, I might be worried. You said yourself this is probably going to be a waste of time. Let's go to the meeting place. If there's the slightest hint of anything, we'll get out of there. I have my cell phone.'

'Yeah, right. If we have a problem, you can call 911.'

Give the woman credit for fortitude. Four years as a deputy prosecutor and as many handling a variety of tricky lawsuits had toughened her hide. She also worked out regularly and had taken self-defense classes, but Kung Fu wasn't going to impress a thug with a gun. At the slightest hint of anything, I planned to set a world land speed record going in the opposite direction. I just wondered if my clunky six-year-old Toyota could outrun a motorcycle.

It was a quarter to ten by the time I headed west down the state road, past the edge of a town, through a succession of prosperous subdivisions, and then along a moonlit asphalt strip between empty fields, stands of trees, and farm fields with soybeans and chin-high corn. The area had once been the stamping grounds of the Ku Klux Klan when the sheeted knights did more stomping than stamping. These days the land was being grabbed up by speculators and developers willing to gamble that the future boundaries of suburbia would spill endlessly southward, creating endless demand for half-million-dollar homes and championship golf courses with names like Paradise Point and Hickory Hollow.

Bronson Road was a paved county road not quite in the middle of nowhere, but close. When I turned, the headlights flashed on a series of staked signs announcing the approach of exclusive new home-sites available in abundance. On the north side of the road were signs of excavation for power or water lines, and an empty backhoe had been parked next to a construction shack and a portable toilet. I could see the outline of an abandoned farm home set back behind a thin grove of poplars. There were no lights of any kind. I calculated we had passed the last occupied residence a mile and a half ago. I kept looking for anything suspicious, like a car parked off the road, and saw nothing.

The road meandered for about a half mile and came to an abrupt halt where a new road started on the right with a billboard announcing CANDLEWOOD in elegant black letters. I kicked on the high-beams and slowed to a crawl. A concrete street extended the equivalent of five or six city blocks. On either side, lots were marked with surveyors' stakes, and foundations had been poured for five or six houses. Some driveways already had been marked off with concrete aprons, and there were six short side streets, each apparently leading to cul-de-sacs. A darkened construction office trailer sat just down from the entrance, but the place was otherwise deserted.

I followed the street to the end. The end was a large lot with the basement dug out, and nothing else. If there was any watchman or security, they weren't in sight. In fact, nothing was in sight. Which worried me.

'What now?' Kit said.

I looked at my watch. Ten o'clock on the nose.

'We'll wait a few minutes. I'll keep the engine running. If our man shows, you stay in the car. If he doesn't, we're out of here.'

'Kind of spooky, isn't it? Do you have any kind of weapon?'

'Yeah, two bony fists and two skittish feet. If there's even a smidgen of anything, you strap in, because I'm going to blow out of here at eighty miles an hour.'

'This car won't do eighty. We should have brought mine.'

'Don't insult my car. What it lacks in speed it makes up in character.'

I turned off the lights. The windows were down, and over the hum of the engine I could hear an owl hooting and insects chirping. I was beginning to feel ridiculous. The police had decided to have a little fun, and we were playing along. If some cop had information about Griffo, there were a million safe places to meet in the city. We didn't have to journey to the boondocks, away from civilization and safety, or the illusion of safety.

I turned the radio on low. The station played big band music. Outside, nothing moved. Every time I glanced at my watch another minute had elapsed.

'Oh, oh,' Kit said.

'Oh, oh, what?'

'Look down the street. There's a car stopped, blocking the exit.'

'Shit.'

All I could see was the shape, but the vehicle wasn't facing us or away from us. It was straddled across the pavement, lights out, so we couldn't get through.

'What now?' Kit whispered.

'If someone wants to talk, they'd drive up and talk. I think maybe we'd better get out of here.'

'I second the motion. Be careful.'

'Careful's my middle name.'

The best-laid plans of mice and men sometimes turn men into mice. I don't mind admitting I felt somewhere between nervous and scared, with a dose of regret added for flavoring. It was easy to talk about flying out of the place at high speed. The reality wasn't so simple. At high speed I could endanger Kit. I had to drive to and around the blocking car in a safe, controllable fashion.

We were attorneys-at-law who had a perfect right to be out here at ten o'clock at night, and we didn't have to tolerate any nonsense from anyone. It sounded good in my mind, anyway.

'I'm going to drive directly at the car,' I said. 'Maybe it's our man and he just wants to talk. If not, once I get around him, we'll get out of here lickety-split.'

'I agree.'

I turned the lights on, snapped on the brights, and threw the car into gear. I drove at about ten miles an hour, calculating that the other car was a quarter-mile ahead. If, as I suspected, the man behind the wheel was an off-duty cop having some fun by scaring the hell out of a couple of lawyers, that wasn't so bad. I was trying to think of other possibilities when Kit said, 'Oh, shit.'

'Yeah,' I said, slowing down.

In our bright lights the car revealed itself as a large black four-door sedan, possibly an Oldsmobile with a big engine. It appeared to contain at least four occupants. Two of these people were wearing what appeared to be white hoods.

We were a hundred feet away and closing.

'Think fast, counselor,' I said.

'They wouldn't dare . . . ' Kit blurted, her voice revealing a touch of anger and a touch of shock. 'They wouldn't . . . '

I was trying to listen and calculate at the same time. There appeared to be eight or ten feet on either side of the sedan, not enough space to get past. But I could get by if I drove up the concrete curb and cut across the front part of what some day would be somebody's lawn. The thing was, I would have to make an instant decision.

Or maybe I could just get out of the car and demand that they identify themselves. Not with Kit; not when there was no one around to help in case we needed help.

'Drive around them,' Kit said.

'Just what I plan to do.'

Thirty feet away, I had to make a move. I accelerated and turned the wheel at the same time, aiming to go around the rear of the sedan, where the curb appeared to be lower. As I did, the car's lights leaped to life and it suddenly moved backward.

Kit shrieked and grabbed my arm. I jerked the wheel. To avoid getting hit, I had to pull hard left into the dirt after we bounced over the concrete. My car spun, the wheels spun for a moment, and headlights flashed through the rear window.

'Jesus, Sonny!' Kit said in a raw voice.

'Call 911. These bastards are trying to ram us.'

'You can't be serious!'

As seriousness goes, this rated ten out of ten. I knew it wouldn't do any good to call anyone. I also knew I couldn't let the sedan disable my car. I had to drive like hell. Fear is a great motivator.

I did a wheelie coming off the lawn and

realized I was pointed in the wrong direction. The sedan lights jumped into my rearview mirror, making the decision for me. I hotrodded down the street, heading to the same deadend where we had parked, but lacking a Plan B for the moment.

'Sonny . . . ' Kit said.

'Yeah, I know. Hang on.'

The sedan closed in. I jerked the wheel again. We bounced through surveyors' stakes and plowed through dirt on what would become more new lawns. I wanted to cut off the other car and then cut around it. The driver anticipated the move. He closed more to the left, flashing his lights and blowing his horn.

Kit turned and balanced on her knees so she could see out the back window.

'Three or four of them. All wearing hoods.'

'I hope we didn't interrupt a cross-burning.'

'No jokes, Sonny. Just drive.'

'I am driving.'

We were going back and forth across the street, more or less in a large circle. When I tried to cut to my left to get on the street ahead of the sedan, the driver anticipated the move and cut me off. The next time we came off the dirt, I turned in the opposite direction.

'There's no way out,' Kit said.

'I'll find a way.'

Suddenly the sedan closed in from behind and rammed against my trunk.

Kit was punching numbers on her cell phone. I turned down one of the side streets, saw the cul-de-sac ahead, and accelerated. I felt like we were doing eighty, but the speedometer was closer to sixty. Before the last lot I turned the wheel hard right. We bounced across a stretch of dirt and headed into a clump of bushes. The other lights followed.

I was concentrating so hard trying to find a way out, I missed what Kit said. Then I heard, 'No, I don't . . . Bronson Road or something . . . how would I know? Look, my name is Lake. I'm an attorney . . . no, I don't know who it is. They're wearing hoods . . . no, they're *wearing* hoods.'

I had driven out of Candlewood by driving through a large open space, dodging around bushes and trees, and reaching some kind of moonlit clearing. The sedan stayed behind. Any minute we might crash into a ravine, but I didn't dare stop. I had no idea what lay ahead. I knew what lay behind.

'Goddamnit,' Kit said. She snapped the lid on her cell phone. 'Where are we?'

'Hell if I know. It sure as hell ain't Kansas any more.'

I swerved to avoid a stand of trees and, to my relief, realized there was a winding county road just ahead. When we hit the pavement moments later, I accelerated, and the other lights fell behind for a moment.

'What now?' Kit said.

'We stay on the road until we find a house or something, and hope we don't break our damn fool necks.'

'They're getting closer again. Can't we do something, Sonny?'

'I'm open to suggestions.'

'Stop and face them?'

'Uh-uh, these boys want to play rough.'

There were enough dips and curves so that the headlights behind disappeared for a handful of moments. When the road straightened out for about a quarter-mile, I accelerated as fast as I dared, but I couldn't shake our pursuers.

'I've got an idea,' Kit said. 'Just take a hard right turn.'

'That's a cornfield.'

'I know it's a cornfield. It's a big cornfield. When you turn, turn the lights off.'

'Yeah, right. They'll think a spaceship sucked us into the sky. They'll see us. They'll follow us.'

'And we won't be any worse off than we are now.'

I snapped off the lights and turned right.

We plowed into a wall of corn with the noise of the stalks brushing and banging against the car, as if we were in a carwash that had gone haywire. The impact slowed us down; I didn't want to touch the brakes anyway. We bounced along for eighty to a hundred feet, until the momentum slowed enough to stop the car.

We both turned to look for headlights. Behind was darkness, except for the glow of the moon touching the horizon.

Kit and I listened to each other breathe.

I said, 'I don't think they're following.'

'If they do, let's get out. They'll never find us.'

I turned off the motor. For no good reason, I thought of Cary Grant being chased through an Indiana cornfield.

We waited and listened to the night sounds. I checked my watch every few minutes. Night creatures skittered along the ground nearby, and insects buzzed through the window, but all else was welcome blissful silence.

'I think they're gone,' Kit said.

'I agree.'

'They're probably laughing their asses off.'

'With good reason. But we're not hurt. No damage.'

'Let's try to get out of here.'

With the lights off, I slowly backed up, had difficulty following the path of crushed cornstalks we had created, then felt bare ground leading to the road. There were no signs of the other car. I followed the road in the direction we had been following before, and after a few minutes turned on the headlights.

We reached a two-lane asphalt road a few minutes later. In ten minutes we were approaching the interstate.

'You were right,' Kit said. 'It was a wild-goose chase. I wonder why. Why harass us because we're doing what we're supposed to be doing.'

'I'll ask O'Hara the next time I see him.'

'You did a good job driving. But we were lucky, too.'

'Not so lucky. Our friends were just playing games. If they wanted to get rough, we wouldn't be cruising merrily back to Indy.'

No one followed us. The traffic on the interstate was normal. The traffic on the city streets was normal.

'I'm not going to be able to sleep,' Kit said. 'I'm too worked up.'

'I'll make an appearance, if you want. What time does the hearing start?'

'Nine o'clock. You don't have to.'

I dropped Kit off at her condo, waited to

make sure she got in all right, and drove home. I was more shaken than I wanted her to know, and sorry I had brought her with me.

Everything was quiet in my neighborhood. I locked the door, turned on all the lights, and drank a cold beer while soaking in a hot bath to the soothing sounds of a Beethoven piano sampler. I was tired and jumpy.

Drying off, I jumped when the phone rang.

I picked up the receiver and didn't say anything.

'Sonny, it's me,' Kit said.

'Hey, are you all right?'

'I'm fine. I'm going to bed. I thought of something I want you to think about.'

'Okay, shoot.'

'Shoot is exactly the right word. If Griffo was wearing a protective vest, and we know he was, how did he get a bullet in the chest? Sweet dreams.'

She hung up.

17

It started raining in the middle of the night. The weather front sent thunder crashing through the city's west side and blessed Broad Ripple with a sweet whispery downpour that tapped on the roof with the precision of a jazz drummer.

I lay in bed drifting between past and present, remembering moments like this when Meg and I were curled in each other's arms. But when I let my mind wander, it went to a chilly gray day eight years ago when the destinies of two men brought them together in a fatal urban opera.

I had slept no more than two desultory hours. At three o'clock I gave up and put on a pot of coffee. While the coffee brewed I turned on the TV and began watching the videotape. Yes, Griffo wore a special dark gray police vest. I watched him enter the house again. I wanted him to turn and look at the camera, to stop and not go inside. Instead I saw him in profile, crossing hunched in front of the porch, and then watched his back as he hit the door and stepped into that undiscovered country we all eventually visit.

My brain refused to concentrate. I put on a Rachmaninoff piano concerto to distract my thoughts while I drank two cups of black coffee. After a leisurely shower I tried to watch TV and finally gave up trying to spot anything new. Outside, the rain had stopped. When I looked out to see if the *Chronicle* had arrived, I found yesterday's mail stuck in the chute. A long white envelope had the *Chronicle* logo in the corner. Inside was a single sheet of glossy paper on which four short newspaper stories, all ten years or older, had been copied. There was no note from Bradley Gray.

The first story was the oldest, just a filler paragraph announcing that U.S. Marine John Griffo had returned from Vietnam, where he had earned a Bronze Star and a Purple Heart. The next, fifteen years old, contained seven paragraphs and mentioned Griffo parenthetically. As a neighborhood patrol officer, he had told the county liquor board he knew of no reason why the license for the Merry-Go-Round nightclub should not be renewed, despite the opposition of the neighborhood betterment association. The third story quoted Griffo about the arrests of two men who had perpetrated a string of residential burglaries. None of the other names were familiar. The last item was a routine filing from city hall reporting the board of public safety's rubber-stamping of police department promotions, including Griffo to the detective division.

I weighed these glimpses of biography as I made breakfast. Jeremiah Jackson was a professional criminal who had spent most of his life robbing people, using drugs, and living behind bars at state expense. John Griffo was a war hero who became a public servant and, whatever his shortcomings, died in the line of duty. The contrast did nothing to fuel my enthusiasm for my job. I wondered if I had been making enemies I didn't need on behalf of a man who didn't deserve anyone's sacrifices.

I exercised in the bedroom and dressed in suit and tie. The neighborhood was quiet as I drove away and blended into the rush-hour traffic heading downtown. I had the feeling I was being watched, but nothing suspicious showed up in the rear-view mirror.

When it comes to providing office space for officials and bureaucrats, our state government ranks second to none. The complex of impressive buildings clustered around the old Capitol included a scenic canal, picnic areas, spacious walkways, and rolling greenery. To most of the people who presided here, an area like Dodge City was no more real than

Emerald City in *The Wizard of Oz*. Most politicians only visited the inner city when they had to pass out campaign literature or needed TV time for a speech on gun control.

I parked in a parking garage and walked to the government center where the parole board would meet in forty-five minutes. The hearing room was a large space painted in pastels, with the American and state flags positioned prominently as if history would sanction anything that would happen today. A half-dozen people already had congregated. If there were any protesters, they would be outnumbered by security personnel.

Kit and one of the professors were unloading materials from briefcases on a long table that faced a longer table where the parole board would sit. Kit looked surprisingly fresh. She wore an off-white cotton suit featuring padded shoulders, subtle earth-colored striping, flat-front pants, and a chocolate-brown ruched blouse. She had fashioned her hair so it looked shorter, making her gold quarter-sized earrings more noticeable. Her brown suede shoes matched her buckled purse. The professor nodded at me, and busied himself reading a brief.

'You hardly look like someone who was chased by nasty men wearing flour sacks not a dozen hours ago,' I told Kit. 'How do you do it?'

She laughed lightly and began straightening papers on the table.

'Believe it or not, I slept like a rock. When I woke up, I really felt annoyed by the whole damn thing. I called the Johnson County sheriff's office and filed an official complaint. Believe it or not, they listened. They're going to assign a detective. They may want to take paint samples from your car.'

'I had a feeling you'd do something. What about the hearing? Anything I can do?'

Kit shook her head. 'I talked to the chairman a few minutes ago. They're giving each side an hour. They'll rule at nine o'clock tomorrow morning.'

'Which means that thirteen hours and five minutes later, Jackson will be a dead man no longer walking.'

'Not because we didn't do everything we could. Including answering the question I raised last night. How did a bullet get through Griffo's bullet-proof vest?'

'I'll ask the one man who probably knows the answer. Dickie Buckley.'

'I said I didn't think Buckley would talk. That was a guess. Now I'm positive.'

'I still have to ask.'

The professor signaled Kit. The room had

started to fill up. Three television stations were setting up their gear and testing their lights. A contingent of uniformed police officers arrived, maybe ten in all. Lawyers I knew came in and sat on the fringes. The four board members arrived separately, two of them with a TV reporter walking along and asking questions.

I was standing by myself when I sensed someone next to me. I turned to see a woman staring.

'You're Ritter, aren't you?'

'Yes, ma'am.'

'I'm Johnny Griffo's widow.'

She was a slight thing, in her fifties, with coal-black hair streaked with gray. She wore a plain brown dress, no jewelry, and carried no purse, but had something small in her left hand.

'I'm sorry about your husband,' I said.

Her voice had a shrill note. 'Are you? Then why do you want to destroy his reputation? That's what you're trying to do, isn't it?'

She had approached me to deliver a message, not to hear explanations or even try to understand why lawyers representing men facing death at the hands of the state were compelled to make sure the orderly search for the truth and due process had been fulfilled as much as possible.

'I don't want to destroy his reputation,' I said. 'Nor do I want to hurt anyone.'

Her dark brown eyes probed my face. 'Then why dig into my husband's past? It's bad enough the man who killed him exists on the same planet. Then to hear some attorney wants to delay his execution by looking for dirt on Johnny, it's disgusting.'

'I'm just trying to do my job.'

She opened her fist. I recognized the Bronze Star.

'Remember this,' she said. 'John won it in Vietnam. Remember this while you worry about a criminal's constitutional rights. Jackson has constitutional rights because my husband fought for his country.'

She turned and walked away. All of the police officers were glaring at me. I retreated into the background as the TV lights went on and the chairman announced the opening of the meeting. I saw Mrs Jackson and the Reverend Foster slip into front seats.

Onlookers had gathered around and outside the main door. Larry Lynch stood among them with his arms folded. He wore a hound's-tooth suit cut to form, a blue shirt, and one of those red bow ties politicians like to wear when they want people to think they're as smart as George Will.

Larry put on his trademark smirk of

condescension when he saw me.

I kept my voice low. 'Here to remind the board that the governor's office is neutral?'

'Sonny, poor Sonny. You're such a *suspicious* sort.'

'You can fool Kit, Larry. You don't fool me. You have a heart the size of a pea.'

Larry nodded his head, as if I had recited both a medical fact and a compliment.

'Remember the wise words of Dr Johnson, Sonny. Nothing will be attempted if all possible objections must be first overcome.'

'What the hell is that supposed to mean?'

'Think, dear boy, think. What's more important? To have a governor who can do good for everyone re-elected, or to beat the drum for a man who's spent his entire life committing crimes? Is this logic going over your head?'

'You son of a bitch. You promised Kit.'

'So I did,' Larry smiled. 'She won't believe you, anyway. I have to live in the real world.'

'I wouldn't call a political dung heap the real world.'

Larry whispered, 'Tut, tut, Carson. You do what you have to do, and I do what I have to do. Doesn't Kit look great in white? I'll bet if you look real close, you can see the outline of her panties.'

I am not a violent person. I believe in law,

174

civilized conduct, and our system of justice. But at the moment I had to resist the temptation to shove a briefcase down Larry's throat with enough force to reach his testicles.

For twenty painful seconds, I bit my tongue. Then I backed away.

The sun had come out, and the streets had rings of steam and fog. I drove to the City-County Building, went into the east wing, and took the elevator to the second floor.

In the chief's office, I identified myself for the receptionist and asked for Lieutenant Rosenthal. Two uniformed officers, a man and a woman, stopped typing on their computer keyboards.

'He's at the statehouse,' the receptionist said. 'Can someone else help you?'

'Rosenthal was going to get me John Griffo's personnel file.'

'Oh, yes. Just a minute.'

She was gone four. When she returned she handed me a manila envelope, and turned away as if I no longer existed.

I stood at the desk and deliberately took my time. The envelope contained two sheets, stapled together. It was Griffo's employment record, but not the record of anyone who had worked for the department as long as he had.

There were a dozen entries when there should have been four times as many. There were assignment changes, commendations, comments, and nothing else. If a single complaint had ever been made, it wasn't logged here.

I'm no document expert, but I have two eyes to see things. What I saw looked like something had been deleted and the paper pushed together before it was copied. In effect, part of Griffo's police career had been whited-out.

18

To locate Buckley I had to locate Snookie Edwards. I didn't have far to go. I took the elevator up to the police courts. Edwards was where he always was, in the middle of the action.

Every large courthouse has someone like Snookie. He's the man who knows everything about everybody. He doesn't seem to have a regular job other than doing things for judges, bailiffs, attorneys, bondsmen, private investigators, and cops. He gives advice to people in trouble and steers them to people who can help them out. He cuts corners and red tape. He's a facilitator. Some might call him a fixer.

The hallway outside the municipal courts teemed with humanity. When several courts emptied at the same time it reminded me of a railroad station where wartime refugees stumbled about looking for a friendly face. Most of the people were from those neighborhoods we like to label as lower-class or lower middle-class. Sadly, it looked like a reunion of high school dropouts. These people didn't know it, but they were moving along a conveyor belt the overworked court system had installed just to prevent gridlock. I saw a few lawyers I knew working the corridor. There was never any shortage of clients, just a shortage of clients who would pay their fees.

Snookie had one of his favorite corners, where an elderly man and woman listened intently while Snookie did the talking. He nodded to acknowledge my presence. When the elderly couple went their way, Snookie signaled me with his finger.

He was a short, rail-thin man who was probably seventy-five and managed to look fifty. He had a crown of hair dyed reddish brown, Elvis sideburns with remnants of gray, and a pock-marked face. The voice had a smoky kind of seriousness. Everything Snookie said and did was serious. As far as I knew, Snookie never joked.

'I haven't seen you around here lately, Sonny,' he said as he shook my hand. 'I hear you stepped on a couple of big toes.'

'If I did it was an accident. I'm just trying to earn a living. I'm not interested in causing trouble for anyone.'

Snookie released my hand. 'That's good, that's good. Life's too short to make unnecessary enemies. Come to think of it, what's a necessary enemy?' He puzzled over his own question. 'I hear things, Sonny. I hear you're going to bat for J. J. Jackson.'

'Well, you hear wrong. I'm not going to bat for the man. I'm just making sure no one made any mistakes they might regret after it's too late to do anything about them. I hope you don't have a problem with that.'

Snookie shrugged. 'You do your thing, I do my thing. It's good to see you down here. You were always good for business. Some of these new lawyers, they got their noses stuck in law books. They don't know how things work. You try to tell them, they look at you like you're some kind of cave man. Welcome home.'

'Thanks. I'm looking for Dickie Buckley.'

Snookie's scrawny shoulders shook with mirthful surprise.

'One minute you say you're not looking for aggravation, next minute you bring up Buckley. Sonny, you know cops. I don't have to tell you how thin-skinned they are when it comes to their own. Buckley won't talk to you.'

'Yeah, I know. But I have to hear it from him. I know he's retired. I don't know where he hangs his hat.'

When Snookie had something important to say, he made certain he was facing a wall. He turned and faced the wall. He talked like an amateur ventriloquist trying not to move his lips.

'Dickie's managing a nightclub. He's there most of the time. The Merry-Go-Round, out on Michigan Street.'

Somehow I wasn't surprised. 'He works for Butch Tunney?'

'Sure. I mean, technically, it's not Butch's place. But everybody knows it is. Butch takes care of his friends. Cops retire, they find out their pension don't stretch like they thought it would. You can talk to Buckley, but he won't talk about his partner.'

'I thought Griffo was a model cop. Now I'm hearing otherwise. Stories that aren't very pretty.'

'I don't know about that, Sonny. We all have problems, don't we? Griffo was just like anybody else. But, you know what? He didn't deserve to go down like that. He was a good cop. He just wasn't perfect. Who the hell is?'

'What sort of problems did Griffo have?'

Down the hall, people surged out of a door as one of the courts ended. Snookie drew me closer with a hand flashing three diamond rings.

'He was a boozer, I heard that. Liked the girls. Had trouble with his wife, don't we all. I'll tell you something, Sonny, if you forget where you heard it.'

'I feel a siege of amnesia coming on.'

'He had a thing with Barb Cotton for awhile. Then they split up. Details I don't know. One other thing, which I don't have to tell you. Don't get crosswise with Butch. You know that.'

'I know that.'

'Butch isn't such a bad guy. Tell you what. Big white house behind his club, that's where Buckley lives. For free.'

'People who buy people are the luckiest people of all.'

The line flew right over Snookie's head.

'I gotta go, Sonny. You watch out for yourself. Big toes go with big feet. Big feet have big shoes. Shoes that hurt.'

'Thanks, Snook. If I see Big Foot, I'll run in the opposite direction. Take care of yourself.'

'You, too.'

I took the stairs to the main floor and cut through the tower lobby to the west wing entrance. The sun had disappeared and a thunderstorm pelted the streets, sending everyone to cover. I stood a few feet from the entrance waiting for the rain to die down. The revolving door kept spilling out people who squealed in surprise at the weather.

One was a fat, bald man of close to forty years, most of them probably spent with a pork chop in his fist. He wore a light-blue seersucker suit. I recognized him, and stopped him before he could turn around.

'Terry Moss? You probably don't remember me. Sonny Ritter.'

The name tumbled through his memory. His gray-green eyes told me he didn't like what he remembered.

'Sure, Ritter. How you getting along?'

'Just fine. I'm working on the appeal for Jeremiah Jackson. I'd like to ask you a question.' Before he could say no, I continued 'You represented Griffo's wife in a divorce action. I wonder if you can give me some idea of what that was all about.'

Moss wiped his thin lips with a puffy hand to show me he had just tasted something he didn't like.

'You know better than that. Even if I remembered, I couldn't tell you anything without the client's permission. If you're on a mission to damage Griffo's reputation, she sure as hell won't cooperate. Neither will I.'

'Thanks. I thought I'd ask anyway.'

Moss wiped his mouth again.

'Can I be candid with you?' Before I could say no, he continued. 'You're the kind of lawyer who gives the profession a bad name. You're pro-criminal, anti-peace officer. You advocate the wrong things for the wrong reasons. You liberal, pot-smoking, cocaine-sniffing attorneys make me sick.'

Porky, smug, right-wing deputy prosecutors make me sick in turn, I thought. What I said was, 'You're entitled to your opinion. For what it's worth, I haven't smoked pot since college, and I've never used cocaine. Yeah, I made a mistake. One mistake. And I've paid for it plenty. Like anyone else, I'm entitled to a second chance.'

Moss decided to brave the rain to get away from the likes of me. He lifted his black briefcase over his hairless head.

'So you say. You're not going to prove it by asking other lawyers to breach the confidentiality of a murdered officer's widow. Goodbye.'

He dashed into the rain, and his valise and self-righteousness kept him dry.

19

Bail-bond offices were clustered around the City-County Building like pilot fish around a whale shark. To find Barbara Cotton, all I had to do was cross at the light and walk into the ground-floor office on Market Street.

In the front part, one of the agents, a burly man whose upper arms were covered with bright tattoos, sat in a rocking chair reading the *Chronicle* while the legless man who sold newspapers on the corner by the City Market shined his shoes. I could see Barb talking on the telephone behind her desk in the cluttered back office. She recognized me, and waved me in.

'Look, no more excuses,' Barb said into the receiver. 'Your brother's here by six o'clock tonight or by nine o'clock tomorrow I'll file foreclosure on your house. No more bullshit, darling.'

She hung up and grinned at me.

'They never change, Ritter. Always the same song and dance. I ain't seen him in a month of Sundays, or he's coming over for supper tonight, or just give him a couple of more days and he'll come up with the dough, word of honor. I swear, there isn't a living human being who wouldn't lie through their teeth to the pope.'

'I'd rather have the Terminator after me than you, Barb,' I said.

Barb smiled at the compliment.

'It's that guy out front. Best bail agent in the state. Claims he's got Indian blood, and it wouldn't surprise me.' She fired up a cigarette with a silver Zippo. She had always been a chain-smoker who couldn't go twenty minutes without lighting up. 'Back in the saddle again, eh? I hope you'll be bringing me business.'

Barb was sixty, gray-haired, fairly well-preserved, and as tough as the leather on an old football. Married and divorced four or five times, she had been the top woman in the bail-bond business for the last three decades. And made a lot of money. The shelves behind her desk were filled with model sports and luxury cars of all makes, and she had three or four of the real things in her garage.

'I hope to,' I said to give her reason to be cooperative. 'The phone's starting to ring again. In case you haven't heard, I'm working on the Jeremiah Jackson appeal.'

Barb blew smoke through her nose. She had quick brown eyes skilled at spotting angles and gimmicks on people's faces.

'Someone has to do it, I suppose,' she said without feeling. 'He deserves to die for killing a good man. Too bad they don't cook them like they used to do. Or draw and quarter them. For someone like Jackson, I'd pay for a ticket. Don't try to fool me, Ritter. You're here for a reason.'

I shoved some papers aside and sat in the only other chair.

'I'm back tracking. Nothing serious. I see no reason why the state won't exact the big penalty. But I have a few questions. About Griffo, mostly.'

'I can't tell you much. The man had balls as big as grapefruits. Johnny was a package, he was.'

'I hear you had a thing with him once.'

Barb didn't flinch or react in any way. She studied my face for a moment, no doubt trying to assess how much I already knew.

'Yeah, once upon a time,' she said. 'It was fun while it lasted. But, I'll tell you, Johnny was a handful. Moody, drank too much, violent temper. A good cop, though.'

'Wife troubles, I hear.'

'Hell, seventy percent of the officers have wife troubles, twenty percent have husband troubles, and the other ten percent, well, I wouldn't want to play their softball team. What's the point, anyway? He tried to serve a warrant and Jackson shot him down like a dog.'

'Maybe.'

'Maybe? Don't you watch TV? I cried, damnit. Boy, did I cry. You don't like to see anything happen to a man you've had in your bed, even if he was a bit of a crackpot.'

'In what way?'

Barb crushed her cigarette and lit a fresh one.

'I don't know. Suspicious, you know what I mean? Just because we had a little thing, he'd tail me sometimes, watch me. Then when he thought his wife was getting the deep-six from his partner, boy, did he hit the ceiling. I'm sure Dickie never gave her a second look. Those two were like brothers. Dickie was never the same since. Since the shooting, I mean.'

'You're sure Buckley wasn't humping Griffo's wife?'

'Not Dickie. He had too many other honey pots on the line to mess with Johnny's woman.'

'Why would Griffo think he was?'

'Search me. Like I said, he was the suspicious type. Anyway, I know they made up. Dickie and him.'

The phone rang. Barb listened for a minute and told the caller to come to the office in the morning. As she talked, she looked at me, and her eyes told me to be careful with every step I took.

When she hung up I said, 'I hear Buckley works for Butch Tunney.'

Barb shrugged. 'Sometimes it seems like half the town works for Butch. I like Butch. He refers business to me. He remembers what it was like when he was writing bonds.'

'Funny how Butch used to use Jerusalem Sterne and Jackson ended up with Sterne as his attorney.'

'Is it? Maybe it's not funny at all. An attorney can have a hundred clients without any of them meeting the other. You ought to know that.'

'I do know that. I know this court system is like a tropical reef full of plants and fish that feed off of each other. Like you used to handle bail for Sterne's clients, maybe at the same time Tunney did.'

Barb smiled to show she could be patient. 'Look in the yellow pages and count the agents. If they've been around any time at all, they've worked for the same attorneys.' She tapped ash into a glass tray with a small mountain of butts. 'I like you, Ritter. One thing about you, you're not afraid to work. But I'll feel better after Jackson shuts his eyes permanently.'

'You know anything about J.J.?'

Barb almost hooted. 'Do I know anything about Jackson? I hope to tell you. I bailed his ass out three or four times. You can say this for him, he didn't skip. Let me tell you something about Jackson, honey. They made a big thing about how he never used his gun. But it was just a matter of time. The way he and Mason operated, stick up a place every few nights, one of those nights something was going to happen and somebody was going to get shot.'

'You're probably right.'

'It's just too bad it had to be Johnny. They don't make them like that any more. He was old-school.'

'Old school how?'

'Old school, you know. Get the job done and don't worry about the fine points. Old school. Tough.'

'Some of the old-school cops live by their own rules, Barb.'

She bobbed her head to let me know creative rule-making was part of the real world.

'I got a friend, runs a bar over on Washington Street. Pretty tough joint. Tough customers. One time, he had one mean son of a bitch raising hell and couldn't get rid of him. So he makes a call. A policeman comes over. The policeman walks up to this tough guy and before he knows it, shoves the barrel of his gun in his mouth, and cocks the trigger. And he tells the tough guy something like, 'You're going to leave here now quietly, and you're never going to come back.' The tough guy nods. The cop takes the gun out and the tough guy disappears pronto with his tail between his legs. End of problem.'

'I presume he didn't read him his rights.'

'See, Ritter, that's old school. Get the job done. Johnny was like that. It's a disappearing breed. What the public doesn't understand is just how mean and vicious and back-stabbing half the people walking the streets are. They'll sucker-punch you to steal your tie, or stick a shiv in your back because you looked sideways. It takes guts to go up against that. First in, always. Cops nowadays, well . . . '

'I'm sorry if I opened old wounds, Barb.'

She crushed out the cigarette and laughed in a derisive way.

'The scars are thicker than a rhinoceros's hide. Every year I get a little older and they get a little thicker.'

20

The storm went eastward and the sun came out. The steam followed. Driving out New York Street, I kept the air conditioner full-blast and listened to the radio. There was a live report from the Capitol. The parole board had listened to arguments over Jackson's clemency petition and would announce a decision in the morning. Several lawyers paid to give their opinion opined that the board would vote unanimously to deny Jackson.

The Merry-Go-Round was on a one-way street on a corner between a forlorn residential area and a dying industrial park. Across the street, both the old hotel and the older gymnasium were boarded up. A used furniture store, a variety store, and a service station were the only nearby businesses. Otherwise, small frame residences lined the street with the occasional ten-year-old car parked in front.

From the outside the Merry-Go-Round looked more like a neighborhood laundromat than a nightclub. It was a story-and-a-half, brick-and-concrete building, painted mostly white. A window ran across the front, but green paint on the inside blocked any view. In clumsy, hand painted letters GIRLS GIRLS were announced and Lingerie Lunches promised.

I drove around the back twice and checked the alley. The place had two rear entrances, one into the club and the other presumably into Tunney's private lair. The graveled parking lot was about half-full, perhaps twenty cars, a few bearing out-of-state plates.

Across the alley was the rear of an imposing three-story house, its white paint blotched and cracked. Wild vines and poison ivy covered most of the rickety fence. The gate with several slats hanging loose was open. It was attached on one side to the fence and on the other to a barn-like garage whose neglected exterior needed as much attention as the house.

I parked next to the gate and looked around. Nothing moved. I put my car in park and got out, walking quickly to the side of the garage, just inside the gate, where the beat-up door had a dusty three-pane insert of glass. There was one car inside, a dark blue Buick of uncertain vintage. It was parked in such a way that I could see a kind of rusty discoloration on the front, just above the bumper. I had seen this car before. I had seen it at a place called Candlewood.

I climbed back in my car, swung around front, and parked on the one-way street. Before I went in, I told myself that no matter what happened, there was no point in getting into any verbal duels over Jackson, especially when the end of the line was so near.

Places like the Merry-Go-Round have a unique odor, the pungent aroma of alcohol, tobacco, cleaning solvent, and lust. The smell is like discarded furniture that's been sitting around a stuffy warehouse. Instead of used furniture, the Merry-Go-Round sold used bodies.

The bar ran across the wall in front of the window. The stage spread out from one end in a kind of cloverleaf pattern with two runways extending through the tables. The lights were a kind of shadowy orange designed to reveal some things and conceal others. The brightest thing in the place was the jukebox, and the loudest was the music from the jukebox. It was loud enough to inspire the two mostly naked women who were gyrating in front of the busiest tables.

The two busiest tables each had four businessmen who were clutching schooners of beer and leering happily. A dozen other tables had occupants, all pairs and singles. Only two customers were women. One I didn't recognize; she was a mousy, middle-aged woman who looked like she had her doormat out for any warm male body to trip on. The other I remembered, because I once represented her after one of her forty-million prostitution arrests. Francie was a brassy fifty-year-old who had seen more penises than Dr Spock. She looked at me without recognition or interest.

I ordered a glass of beer and told the bartender who I was and who I wanted to talk to. While he weighed the information, I turned and watched the dancers. One was a fleshy woman with Turkish features and black hair that looked like it had been wetted with syrup. She was twirling her rather enormous breasts in a way that made the customers make wet noises.

I watched the other dancer. She was a bottle blonde on top and a natural blonde down below. She was fortyish, thin, and had pert breasts with nipples the size of young plums. She had something the other dancer didn't have. On her left thigh was a tiny tattoo of a plant with two green blades and white flowers — Venus's-flytrap.

Venus recognized me, mouthed my name with her lips, and moved her finger to encourage me to come closer. When I looked around, the bartender had disappeared. I took my beer to a table and watched Venus orbit. The faces of the men focusing on her were locked in goatish concentration.

When the music ended she stepped down from the stage and jiggled to my table.

'Sonny! How did you know I was here?' She kissed me on the cheek.

'I didn't. I came here to talk to your boss, Dickie.'

She seemed genuinely pleased to see me, but the name brought a frown to her mouth.

'He's not the boss, thank god. Butch's the boss. Dickie I don't care for.' A smile popped out. 'You look *great*, Sonny. You look like a lawyer. Do you like my dancing? What happened to that client of yours?'

'You are a veritable Isadora Duncan, Venus. My client solved his own problem, more or less.'

'Hey, if I need a lawyer, I'll hire you. Do you want to get together again, you know, for a little fun?'

'I didn't know you were a dancer.'

'Part-time. Mostly I model. Lingerie.' She pointed to her black garter belt, in case I didn't know what lingerie was. 'I fill in at clubs when one of the girls is sick. Like this place. Kind of dead here, isn't it?'

Her expression changed into a frown, suggesting things were about to liven up.

She was watching the man approaching from the bar, and I turned to recognize Buckley moving our way like a water buffalo charging a tourist.

'I'd better mingle with the other customers,' Venus squealed. 'I'll call you, okay?'

'Okay.'

Buckley had put on weight, mostly around the waist, the bulk of a man who had been making up for lost time at the dinner table. He had jet-black hair, a fleshy face, and eyes incapable of smiling. He wore a white shirt and slacks. I hardly saw any of this. I was staring at the expensive gold watch on his left wrist. It looked like the kind that cost around twenty thousand dollars.

Buckley sat down next to me.

'I don't know why you're wasting time here, Ritter. You must have missed the noon news. The state's going to punch your client's ticket.' He leaned closer and spoke in a hard, low voice. 'Ever see a man die? You want to know what it's like to watch your partner die? You want to know what it's like leaning over him listening to the blood gurgle?'

My recollection was that Buckley had been too busy kicking Jackson to listen to anything. I didn't say anything. I was shocked Buckley was taking the time to make a speech.

He took out a pack of cigarettes and lit one.

'Jackson's going to get what he should have got eight years ago. I feel good about it. You lawyers, you try to twist everything. You don't care about victims. You don't care about police officers. Well, this time you're going to lose. I'm going to celebrate. You want to drink some champagne with me?'

'No, thanks,' I said as evenly as possible.

'Oh, I forgot. You're not a drinker, you're a coke freak.' He snorted. 'Pardon the breach of etiquette.'

He signaled the bartender. I waited politely. Buckley ordered a champagne cocktail, and turned back to me.

'You must be anxious to hurry up to Michigan City so you can hold that killer's hand. That's fine with me. Can we do something for you? You like the dancers, eh?'

'I want to ask you a couple of questions, if you don't mind.'

'No, I don't mind. Does that surprise you? I can see it does. Well, I'm in a good mood. I'm going to relax and get ready to sit up in the prison and watch Jackson close his eyes and go bye-bye. You must've read my testimony. I'm not going to tell you anything different.'

'*You're a dead man*. Any chance Griffo

said that instead of Jackson?'

Buckley stared at me as if I might start raving.

'John wasn't stupid. Maybe he had more guts than brains, but when he faced an automatic, he wouldn't make speeches.'

The bartender brought Buckley's drink and a refill for me. I tried to pay, and Buckley waved him off.

I said, 'You're . . . a . . . dead . . . man. It takes Jackson what, two seconds to say. Enough time for Griffo to shoot first.'

'Listen carefully, Ritter. I was there. I heard it. So did other officers. It happened bang, like that. You blink and it's over. You must have seen the thing on TV.'

'Seen, yes. You can't hear much.'

He leaned closer with gritted teeth.

'You heard Jackson's gun, didn't you? That's all you needed to hear. The gun that killed a good cop. My partner. Now you, you're trying to tear him down. Asking a lot of stupid questions.'

I could see Buckley was working himself into a fit of indignation.

'I'm just doing my job,' I said calmly.

Buckley's voice suddenly became the equivalent of a Doberman growling through a muzzle.

'And John was just doing his job. You know

how old he was?' Buckley's fat hand clamped on my wrist. 'He was forty-six. Think about that. Forty-six. And asshole attorneys like you want to piss on his grave.'

'Asshole attorneys like me wonder how your partner got shot in the chest when he was wearing a bulletproof vest.'

The question touched a landmine somewhere in Buckley's rage. I thought his eyes might pop out of the sockets.

'What difference does it make?' he said in a spray of spit. 'John took two in the head. He was dead in an instant. You ever seen someone shot in the head?'

The last question was not meant to elicit an answer. It was a verbal launching pad that would bring Buckley out of his chair in two seconds. But he didn't get the chance.

Butch Tunney touched Buckley's shoulder.

'Dickie, why don't you go back to the office? I'll take care of the customers.'

The transformation was instantaneous. The Doberman had just received a command from its trainer. Buckley finished the drink, crushed the cigarette, and walked away.

'You probably don't remember me,' Tunney said. 'I remember you when you were a snot-nosed P.D. working twenty hours a day. I always liked your style.'

Tunney was shorter than I remembered.

He wore a brown suit, a white linen shirt, and a bolo tie. I remembered his eyes. They were like lumps of dark glass.

'I do remember you, Mr Tunney.'

'Good. Listen, you can understand why Dickie's a little on edge. Johnny was a super guy. When Johnny died, we all got hurt.'

'I understand.'

'You'd better be on your way. But, tell you what. Come back next week. Come back any time. I run a fun club. You can have a good time. I'll guarantee it. No one'll hold any grudges.'

Tunney had put his hand on my shoulder in a friendly way. I got the message. I even let him shake my hand.

I had a hundred questions I wanted to ask, but he was telling me to get the hell out while the getting was good.

'Good to see you, Mr Tunney,' I said. 'You run a fine establishment.'

21

I had a prickly, uncomfortable feeling, and the afternoon humidity didn't help. The air conditioner cooled me off and cooled me down. Driving towards downtown, I stopped at a family diner for a late lunch. When I finished eating and meditating over a second cup of coffee, I went to the phone booth on the corner and called Kit on her cell phone.

'This is Katherine Lake.'

'Sonny. I hear the parole board doesn't look promising. You must be pretty down.'

'Down? Sonny, I'm pissed off, pardon my French. We always use 'arbitrary and capricious' in our pleadings. Now I know what the words really mean. I'm starting to hate smug bureaucrats. I don't know, it was just so annoying. Did you talk to Buckley? Are you all right?'

'I'm all right. I talked to Buckley, more or less. He wouldn't give me much other than his indignant cop speech. The guy gives me the creeps. I don't trust him.'

'I was worried he might try something rough with you.'

'He would have but for the presence of his

employer. Fellow named Tunney.'

'Buckley works for Tunney?'

'Manages his nightclub. The most interesting thing I picked up didn't come from Buckley. Came from a woman I know. She says there was a time when Griffo thought Buckley was having an affair with his wife. That Griffo blew his top. She thinks Buckley wasn't, and they made up. If you like conspiracy theories . . . '

There was a five-second pause before Kit said, 'Are you thinking what I'm thinking? No, that's impossible. At least I think it's impossible. Tell me it's impossible.'

'It's impossible.'

'So more fascinating but irrelevant information, for our purposes, anyway. What else?'

'That car that chased us into the cornfield is sitting in the garage behind Tunney's club. I'll bet you it's registered to Buckley.'

'I'll notify the Johnson County sheriff. Maybe they can test the paint.'

'Okay, but don't get your hopes up. They're not going to go after a retired Indianapolis cop without a barrel full of evidence.'

'I suppose. What else?'

'I got a copy of Griffo's personnel file. It doesn't show a single complaint. Looks like it's been doctored. Or they just doctored the copy they gave me.'

'That's outrageous. The question is, what are they trying to hide?'

'Complaints about beatings, maybe. I don't know. I'm not sure it matters, either. Anyway, I'm out on the east side, so I'm going to look up J.J.'s old girlfriend on the off chance she's still around. I'll call you tonight.'

'No,' Kit said, 'let me call you. I'm meeting with Mrs Jackson. We have to prepare for tomorrow. She wants us to go up to the prison with her. I'm not sure I'm ready. I managed to convince myself there wouldn't be an execution.'

'You've given it your best shot, Kit. You should have no regrets.'

'Somehow I don't find that comforting.'

It was only a ten-minute drive to the house. There were brown patches where there had been lawn, and a row of marigolds lined the porch. The place looked shabby, partly because the front gutter and downspout were hanging by nails, partly because of the cracked glass in the downstairs windows.

An elderly woman answered the door but talked through the screen. Tanya Byrd, Jackson's old girlfriend, had moved to Detroit five or six years ago. No, she had no idea how to contact the woman. I thanked her and drove away.

I caught the vanguard of rush-hour going

north. It was sunny and hot again, and most of the cars had the windows closed. I sat at the traffic lights wondering what I needed to do that I hadn't done. When I reached Broad Ripple, I went down the avenue and pulled into the lot outside Star Liquors.

Leland Hurt was behind the counter. He wore a suede vest over his white shirt, with the sleeves rolled up, and chewed on a toothpick. His glance said he recognized me.

I picked up a bottle of Cutty and stood behind two customers. When the others left I paid for the purchase and said, 'How's your memory, Mr Hurt?'

'A good memory is a blessing and a curse.' He gestured over his shoulder at a small color TV sitting on top of a beer case. 'I didn't see you on the news today. A rather attractive woman who reminds me of my daughter spoke for Jackson. Not that it'll do any good.'

'Kit Lake, my associate. She does the brain work, I do the foot work. I was wondering if you remember the name Butch Tunney.'

Hurt's burst of laughter revealed sarcasm as well as humor.

'Do I remember the name Butch Tunney? Why do you come in here trying to open doors that have been shut for years? I'll say this for you, Mr Ritter. You are persistent. It's a good quality. Used to have it myself.'

A woman came in to pick up a bottle of gin, and examined me with eyes that spoke of lonely days and lonelier nights. She walked out with no response other than the tinkling bell.

'You didn't answer my question,' I told Hurt.

'Well, if it'll get rid of you, yes, I know the name. Matter of fact, I wrote a lot about the man. You'd know that if you'd take the trouble to check the clips.'

'I checked the clips on Griffo. It didn't occur to me to check on Tunney. Griffo was on Tunney's payroll.'

Hurt raised his silvery eyebrows. 'He was one of them, was he? Not surprising. Tunney had a lot of people working for him. Yes, I did three or four stories on Tunney, maybe fifteen or twenty years ago. Nasty fellow. He looks harmless, but he'd kill you without blinking. Or have you killed.'

'What were your stories about?'

'Oh, we were writing about organized crime. Butch had never really been given his due. Didn't come to anything. I think I won an award and moved on to the next project. I interviewed Tunney once, in his saloon. Lied through his teeth. I had a detective friend of mine sitting nearby with a Colt stuck in his belt.' Hurt smoothed his moustache, letting

205

the memories flow back. 'As I recall, Tunney made a half-ass threat to sue me. But he really didn't give a damn. A little bad publicity, and then it all blew away. The FBI was after him one time, I remember. Nothing ever came of it.'

'How'd you get on Tunney in the first place?'

'I don't mind telling you. I had a friend in a certain federal agency, not the FBI. The friend had an informant, a woman who worked for Tunney. He arranged a sit-down. She had a ton of information. Knew about some murders. Nothing much was ever done, though. Tunney had too many influential friends.'

A man came in and started examining the beer cooler.

'So what's your point?' said Hurt. 'The world will hardly notice it when your client gets launched into eternity, as the old-timers used to put it.'

I waited while Hurt sold a case of beer. When the man left I said, 'Jackson's not quite dead yet.'

Hurt harrumphed. 'Tell you something. I witnessed an execution, back in '60 or '61. Man named Kiefer. Killed his wife and daughter. The state electrocuted him. It made a pretty good story, and it was an experience

I didn't care to repeat, seeing a fellow get cooked so his skin steams. Anyway, back then nobody paid much attention. Oh, we had a front-page story, but there weren't any protests, bishops wringing their hands, candlelight vigils, editorials, none of that crap. No, it was cook 'em and forget 'em. Your man's getting off a lot easier. Although I did read an article that some of these lethal-injection procedures don't end up as quite the nighty-night-don't-let-the-bedbugs-bite executions the death-penalty folks claim they are.'

'Jackson's not getting off easier if there's some reason he shouldn't be executed in the first place.'

Hurt shook his head. 'That's for you lawyers to argue so you can run up your billable hours.'

'Maybe you can explain why you called Jackson's attorney two weeks before the trial.'

'Did I? I don't know that I did. Anyway, I'm not a player, and I don't want to be.'

'Not even for the sheer hell of it?'

The question struck Hurt right in the funny bone. His upper body shook with what I thought was mirth but realized was more like the kind of bitter laughter that can melt wax. He cleared his throat.

'On my last day of work they were going to

have cake and punch. I worked there forty-three years, and these so-called editors who wanted to replace me with college kids, they wanted me to have cake and punch with them so maybe they could give me a gold watch or a set of pens. Well, sir, I went out the side door. I'm not a man who likes vulgarity, but I'll tell you what I was thinking. 'Go fuck yourselves.' A phrase perfectly suited for certain occasions, you'll have to admit. Anyway, I hope they choked on their cake and punch.'

The urgency crept into my voice.

'Look, anything at all . . . '

'Sorry, Mr Ritter.'

'I'll be back,' I promised.

A car I didn't recognize was parked in front of my house. It was a red Ford Mustang, six or seven years old, showing rust around the rocker panels. One of the tires was a balding blackwall. As I stepped on the porch I noticed the front door was open. Venus waved when I opened the screen door.

'Hi, Sonny. Is that something to drink?'

She was wearing a one-piece red dress and had her hair pinned up. She looked wanton, delicious, and available. But I was in no mood.

'Venus, how did you get in?'

'The key under the flowerpot. I looked

under the mat first.' She put her hands on my shoulders. Her eyes had a kind of nervous desperation. 'You don't mind, do you? I was thinking, like last time.'

'I do mind, honey. I'm hot and tired and . . . preoccupied. Maybe some other time. Why don't you leave your number?'

'Gee, Sonny, are you sure? A couple of drinks and Venus will make you forget your troubles.' Her voice had a squeaky note of pleading.

'Some other time, Venus. I mean it.'

She gave me a pouty look before she went to the couch and picked up her purse. She primped her hair as she passed the mirror by the door.

'Okay, if that's what you want. See you around.'

'Take care of yourself.'

'Gots to. You know, look out for number one.'

I watched her walk to her car and drive away. I remembered the night Curry died. Everything was so screwed up right now, I didn't think even Venus could distract me. Besides, I expected Kit to call and probably want to get together.

I turned on the window air conditioners, filled a glass with Cutty, tossed my suit coat and shoes in the bedroom, and checked the refrigerator for something to eat. There was a plastic container of week-old pasta salad and two slices of pizza so hard a hacksaw couldn't cut them. I drank a big glass of orange juice and went into the living room to watch TV and sip Scotch.

I had the sound muted during a commercial. A car drove by. A lawnmower puttered down the street. A dog barked, and another dog yapped. A jet rumbled high above. Bugs made noises in the trees.

Then everything happened at once.

Someone kicked the screen door in.

Loud voices yelled, 'Search warrant! Search warrant!'

More voices yelled, 'Down! Down! Get on the floor, motherfucker!'

Feet were pounding on the porch and in the kitchen.

I saw a blur in a flak jacket and helmet pointing an automatic rifle at me. That's all I saw because a second later I was face down, nose into the carpet, with a shoe on my neck, my arms behind my back, and pieces of cold metal being snapped on my wrists.

'Situation secure,' someone said.

I could see three sets of black shoes.

'Okay, okay,' another voice said. 'Get him up.'

Hands lifted me up roughly.

'Read him his rights.'

'I know my . . . ' I started to say.

'Read him his rights. I want this by the book.'

There were at least eight cops in the house. Three were in the living room, two with weapons pointed at me. One of them read my rights. Another was Lieutenant Rosenthal, who glared at me as if I had been caught cannibalizing a newborn baby.

'Look,' I started to say.

'Carson Ritter,' the lieutenant said, 'you are being arrested on charges of possession of narcotics with intent to distribute. We are videotaping this procedure in order to guarantee due process in all respects. Even though you are an attorney, I want to advise you to say nothing until you talk to an attorney. Do you understand?'

'Yes.'

A voice called from the bedroom. 'It's here, lieutenant. Bring the camera.'

Except for my guardians, everyone rushed towards the bedroom. I stood in the middle of the living room in shock. My stomach had disappeared into some other part of my body. I was trembling.

Two minutes later, Rosenthal returned, followed by his entourage. He held a bag of white powder slightly smaller than a soccer ball.

'Ritter, we found cocaine in your bedroom. This confirms informant information that you are dealing major weight. I want to give you the opportunity to identify any more of your stash before we search the premises pursuant to warrant.'

I said, 'I've never seen that before. It was planted. I've been set up.'

The lieutenant couldn't keep the sarcasm out of his voice.

'Sure. Get him out of here.'

22

Under our system of jurisprudence, you are presumed innocent unless and until you are found guilty. It's an important constitutional protection, wrapped in the red, white, and blue bunting of legal history. There's just one little hitch they don't teach you in civics class. You are presumed innocent, but you're *treated* as if you're guilty.

Most law-abiding citizens don't learn this subtle distinction until it's too late. Usually the revelation arrives when they feel a boot on the back of their neck or they're ordered to flatten themselves face-down on a cold pavement while fully loaded weapons are aimed at their bodies. Then they're handcuffed and taken to a lockup, where they probably will be strip-searched. They discover how humiliating it is to stand naked in front of strangers and, when directed, to spread their buttocks. If the strangers so desire, they have the authority to stick a finger up your rectum, in search of contraband. In my case, they settled for making sure I didn't have a revolver hidden in my mouth.

The law-abiding citizen stuck in jail

discovers that other prisoners really run the show. For hours, he sits in a holding pen, breathing the stench of sweat and urine. He begins to realize his custodians look upon him in the same way butchers look upon carcasses rolling down a packing house production line. The custodians, however, are invisible. They watch their prisoners via closed-circuit television.

You hope they're watching, anyway. Especially if you're sharing an overcrowded common cell with a colorful assortment of stickup artists, drug dealers, drunks, and crazies, including burly men decorated with tattoos who seek to relieve their boredom by telling you how much they liked the rape scene in *Deliverance*.

Of course you can make a phone call. You can make a phone call when they decide you can make a phone call, providing you can get by any of the fifty people, most of them unfriendly, who are waiting to use one of the four phones and probably wondering how they flunked their anger management classes. You also have to have the money to make the call, because such a call is likely to cost five or ten times as much as any other phone. If you have to call collect, you'd better hope a machine doesn't answer, because a machine doesn't take collect calls.

You can also make bail. You can make bail, once the bail commissioner arrives to set the bail, or you finally get to court for a preliminary hearing. Of course the paperwork occasionally will disappear. That can add some extra hours. In fact, you can spend a couple of days behind bars before you ever get the opportunity for release, assuming you can meet the cash or surety bond.

I knew the drill. I also realized someone was taking great care to make sure my processing followed every rule. No one said a word as they took my fingerprints; no one made any comment while I was being photographed. I was allowed to make my call from the sergeant's office. I listened nervously to the ringing and then heard Kit's recorder click on. I left my message, and hoped Kit would hear it sooner rather than later.

Then I had plenty of time to sit on a cold bench and contemplate how efficiently I had been set up. It was so good, I couldn't find any flaws. It was so good, I had to face the realization that I could be convicted, sent to prison, and disbarred.

All my bravado had disappeared. Fear and worry will do that.

The pen had gray walls, benches, metal urinals, and two toilets. Through the bars I could see a larger holding area with metal beds, all of them occupied, and men sitting on floors. There were twenty-one men in my area, most of them black. They left me alone, probably because I looked like someone who might be important.

There were no windows, no calendars and no clocks. I sat up all night and knew morning had arrived when two deputies escorted a trusty to the door for the distribution of breakfast. The brown paper bag had a baloney sandwich, a wrinkled piece of cheese, and a carton of milk. I wasn't hungry anyway.

I knew there were two hearing courts, one in the morning and one in the afternoon. I got the late one, which at least allowed me to doze off for an hour or so. Two deputies arrived and called our names. I joined eight men who were attached to a common chain. I knew the route. We would take a jail elevator upstairs to court.

We came off the elevator into a holding area. Three bailiffs waited, and so did two television crews. Each crew had a man holding a camera and a blonde-haired woman holding a microphone.

They approached me in a glare of lights.

'Mr Ritter,' one of them said, thrusting the microphone at my mouth. 'The police identify you as a major Broad Ripple cocaine dealer. Do you have any comment?'

Any attorney would tell me to shut up. My brain told me to shut up. Then I thought of my father and mother and Meg.

'I'm completely innocent,' I said, giving them a sound bite. 'The charges are absurd.'

'Officers confiscated cocaine from your house,' the other blonde said. 'How do you account for that?'

'I'm completely innocent,' I repeated. 'I don't sell drugs and I don't use drugs.'

'Then how did cocaine get into your residence?'

'When all the facts come out, you'll know the answer.'

The first blonde pushed closer. 'How long have you been selling cocaine? Do you sell to school children?'

'I stand by my statement,' I said, and turned my head.

They were satisfied. They had enough to run and re-run tape of this dangerous lawyer in the custody of the guardians of justice. The bailiffs and deputies could barely suppress their sniggers.

The door opened. The TV watchdogs went out, and we were unhooked from the chain.

I could see the municipal courtroom wasn't as busy as usual. We were nudged out the door and into a box of seats to the judge's left. To my relief, I saw Kit approaching the attorneys' table. To my disgust, I saw Terry Moss at the prosecution table. He stared at me with a smug Porky Pig look.

Kit managed a wan smile. She had dark circles under her eyes.

I recognized a face in the front row. My father nodded his head slightly. I nodded back. I felt a surge of emotion.

I knew the judge by reputation. He was a perennial appointee known to have the worst toupee in civilization, a gray bowl of fake hair that looked like it was on backwards. In the police courts, he was known as the Henry Ford of judges, because he moved things along faster than any production line. He moved things along because he was a golf nut always anxious to get to his country club.

My case was called second. I left the box and stood next to Kit as the judge's clerk recited the cause number and charges.

'Not guilty, your honor,' Kit said before the judge could ask.

'What does the state have to say on bail?'

Moss bounced to his feet. 'We would ask for a million dollars, judge. Defendant is believed to have hidden cash in substantial amounts, plus connections outside the country.'

'That's ridiculous,' Kit snapped. 'The

defendant is an attorney in good standing with ties to the community. He doesn't have any hidden cash. He certainly doesn't have connections outside the country.'

Moss puffed himself up. 'Mr Ritter has a cocaine history, your honor. As for his standing as a lawyer, I wouldn't exactly call it good.'

'Enough, enough,' the judge said. 'This is a preliminary hearing, guys, not a *Matlock* rerun. One hundred thousand, cash or surety. Next.'

'One hundred thousand,' I muttered.

'Don't worry,' Kit whispered. 'It's all been arranged. I'll see you at the booking desk.'

Moss flashed a cat-ate-the-canary grin, and walked away triumphantly.

It took forty minutes to get out of the place. I had to collect my belongings and sign papers. I knew the day sergeant slightly. He was a bald man who seemed to enjoy his work.

'Kind of different from the inside, isn't it?' he said.

'Yeah, it is.'

'Had a guy try to break out last week. The jail you can break out of. This place, no.'

'I'm sure you're right.'

He grinned happily. 'Houdini couldn't breakout of this place. The courtroom, maybe, but not from down here.'

Houdini. Harry Houdini. Famous magician and escape artist. I wondered if I still had a book about Houdini I'd read back in high school. It revealed in detail how Houdini pulled off many of his celebrated illusions.

Kit was waiting in the hallway. She was struggling to hold back tears.

'Sonny . . . I'm so sorry. This . . . '

'Does Meg know? Did you talk to Meg?'

'Yes. She's furious, and very hurt. She understands. She wanted to come with me. I told her I didn't think it was a good idea.'

'I'm glad my father came.'

'He put up the bail. I explained everything to him, Sonny. I mean, I explained to the extent I can.' She took my hand.

'I need a cup of coffee. And a shower.'

Kit looked at her watch. 'I don't have much time. Time for coffee, maybe.'

When we left the building and started crossing the street to the City Market, I noticed a warm blue sunny day without a trace of clouds.

'What time is it, anyway?'

'Just after two. The parole board voted four-zero this morning. The execution will be at five minutes after midnight. I'm riding up with Mrs Jackson and her minister. She still wants you to come, by the way.'

In the cavernous market, we got cups of Blue Mountain coffee and carried them upstairs to the railed mezzanine. The tables overlooked the main floor, which was filled with produce and meat stands and small eateries.

'I read the affidavit,' Kit said as we sat down. 'The police say a confidential informant told them you offered to sell him cocaine. That was the basis for the warrant.'

'Her, not him. I'm almost certain it'll be a woman named Venus. Well, not Venus. Her real name's Heather Campbell. Or so she told me. She's a stripper.'

Kit's frown suggested she was preparing to not like my explanation.

'I met her right before Curry was killed. Strictly coincidence. Picked her up in a bar. We had a few drinks. She came home with me. I forgot about her. Yesterday, when I went to Tunney's place, she was dancing there.'

'She works for Tunney?'

'Not exactly. I think for a service that supplies dancers and models for different places. The Merry-Go-Round's one. Technically, she works for Dickie Buckley. Or did yesterday.'

'Oh, great.'

I sipped coffee. I was starting to feel human again.

'Now, wait a minute, Kit. I ran into her by accident. Buckley saw me talking to her. The way I figure it, they planted the drugs and paid her or coerced her to say I tried to sell to her. Almost certainly the latter. Anyway, she was waiting when I got home, so she'd know the layout of the house. Said she'd let herself in with my spare key, which I believed.'

'A stripper. A coincidence. Your spare key.'

'Well, now I know why the mystery caller invited me out to the boondocks. While they were chasing us around the mulberry bush, someone was inside my house, figuring out where to stash the cocaine. Setting the whole thing up.'

'But *why*?' Kit demanded. 'Jackson's been losing at every stop.'

'Maybe I'm closer to something than I realize. Maybe they just want to send a message to lawyers not to mess with them. Maybe they wanted to make sure the parole board saw my picture in the paper right before voting. Lots of maybes.'

'Sonny, I'm worried. I look at this thing and . . . '

'I know. It's a beaut. Perfect, as far as I can see. Do you think Moss . . . ?'

Kit shook her head emphatically. 'No, no, not him. He may be a pompous prig, but he's basically honest. They would have to bring it to him. He wouldn't be a party.'

'That's what makes it so damned good. I think the narcs probably weren't parties either. Which'll make them better witnesses.' I crushed the coffee cup and sighed until my lungs emptied. 'Sorry, kid. I let this happen. Sorry I let you down.'

'You didn't. This is totally outrageous. I assure you, every resource of Ritter Ritter will be used to fight it. We'll get this thing thrown out. Then you'll sue them for ten million dollars. Twenty million. *We'll* sue them. It's Orwellian. It'll scare the hell out of every lawyer in America.'

'Sure, Kit. We'll win.'

The words were strong. The voice weak.

She said, 'The question right now is, do you want to ride with us to Michigan City?'

I told her no. I needed time to recharge my batteries. Kit said she understood.

'Do me a favor, Sonny. Don't do anything until I return tomorrow. And, please, double please, don't go anywhere near that stripper.'

'Promise. Scout's honor.'

'You're not a scout. Come on, I'll drive you home.'

Kit was quiet on the way to Broad Ripple, probably contemplating the ordeal ahead. She handed me her cell phone as I got out of the car.

'I can't take that inside the prison, so you can't call me. I'll call you, say at six, eight, and ten o'clock. Please, Sonny, get some rest. We'll think of something tomorrow.'

'Yeah,' I said. 'Tell J.J. to send me a postcard from the other side.'

23

The house wasn't the wreck I expected. The screen door needed new hinges and all of the drawers had been emptied and some of the furniture moved, but no walls or floors had been damaged and nothing appeared to be missing.

Wandering from room to room, I felt wounded and vulnerable, as if some private part of me had been violated. I couldn't put off the fear that someone was hiding in the house, or a listening device had been planted. When I checked everything and found nothing, I began to wind down.

I took a hot shower and put on my running clothes. The blazing summer sun felt good. The humidity worked to steam out the clamminess from a night in jail. I followed my usual route up and down the boulevard, and didn't see a single cop. They didn't need to waste any more of their time.

When I returned home I took a cold shower. The phone started ringing as I was toweling dry. I wanted to ignore it, but worried Kit might be calling, or maybe Venus with apologies and explanations.

'Hello?'

'Sonny, are you all right?' Meg said. 'I can't tell you how angry I am.'

It was the one voice that could soothe my demons.

'I'm okay, Meg. I'm just getting my second wind. Kit told me you wanted to come to court. Thank you.'

'I know this isn't like the last time. I want you to know that. It's just so . . . unspeakable. Is there anything I can do? I know how you are, Sonny. You'll get depressed and start drinking. I guess I can't blame you.'

'Hey, I'm not going to get depressed and I'm not going to start drinking. I just came in from a run. I'm okay. In fact, I have an idea. Listen, do you remember that book I had on Houdini's magic tricks? Remember what happened to it?'

Meg hesitated. 'Houdini? If I remember right, that was one of the books that were ruined when the water heater burst, remember? Sonny, are you serious?'

'Very much so. You know what? Just talking to you makes me feel better. You know the Ritters. Stiff upper lip, what? Damn the fuzzy wuzzies.'

She laughed lightly. I missed that laugh. The sound was like Mozart at his sweetest.

'I can see you doing your imitation of your father,' she said. 'In an odd way, your dad and I are closer now since the . . . you know. I know what happened today, last night, it's really upset him. And poor Kit, to have to watch a man die.'

'Kit'll be fine. She's a strong girl. Woman. Believe it or not, Meg, I've got to run. David's got one last stone in his slingshot.'

'Be careful, Sonny. Don't get too down.'

She said goodbye.

I put on my lawyer's uniform. I tucked a white silk handkerchief in the breast pocket for added effect. Driving downtown, I realized I was famished. But food would have to wait.

According to the telephone book, Midwestern Security Products was the largest retailer of police equipment in the area, and one of the oldest. It had two buildings on Market Street, under the ramp leading to the interstate highway, about five blocks from police headquarters. One was a wholesale storage facility, the other a retail store filled to the aisles with equipment and paraphernalia: uniforms, hats, shoes, belts, weapons, protective devices, badges, and just about any kind of insignia imaginable.

The salesman introduced himself as Dave and pledged to answer any question. He was a tanned, muscular man of about forty, with slick black hair and a trained smile. He wore slacks and a formfitting, short-sleeved blue knit shirt.

I told him I was interested in body armor.

'What we don't have, we can order and put in your hands within twenty-four hours,' Dave promised, steering me by the arm.

We turned in to an aisle where the shelves and stalls in either direction were filled with vests, jackets, and other types of protective clothing, most of them white, blue, or black.

'What sort of body armor are you interested in?'

'What sort of body armor do you have?'

Dave laughed obligingly at my little joke.

'The very best. We serve most of the major police departments in the state. We have all levels of protection and most manufacturers.'

'What do you mean by levels?'

Dave pointed at different rigs to illustrate his answer.

'Levels are ratings of protection based on standards of the National Institute of Justice. Nowadays, of course, everything has Kevlar, but there are levels of stoppage. A vest that will stop a .44 Magnum with a two-hundred-forty grain bullet won't necessarily stop a knife. We have vests that'll do both.'

'What exactly is Kevlar?'

Dave looked at me as if I might not know what an atom was.

'The wonder fiber DuPont came up with in the 1970s. Stuff was developed to replace steel belts in tires. It's unsurpassed as a ballistic fabric. And when you combine Kevlar with steel armor plate, man, it'll stop a highpowered rifle. What exactly are you looking for?'

'Do you have any of the vests police departments used eight or ten years ago? I think they're a little bulkier than the ones in use today.'

'Ah,' said Dave, steering me by the elbow to a back storage room. 'Surplus. Let me tell you something. The manufacturers' warranties expire at five years. Between us, I think it's a gimmick to move product. Fact is, tests show that old armor is just as good as new.'

There was a rack with a dozen or so vests, black, white, and gray, that looked like the kind Griffo had worn.

I pulled one down. 'What's the difference between these and current ones?'

'Design, primarily,' said Dave. 'The new ones aren't as bulky, and they're lighter. These, you'll notice, have the front slot with the flap. You put them on like a jacket. Shuts with Velcro. Today's vests, all of today's vests, are of the bib apron design.'

'Well, let me ask you a technical question. Say I'm wearing a vest like this and someone standing a few feet away fires a nine-millimeter weapon at me. Will it penetrate the material?'

Dave chuckled. 'Are you kidding? That may be a bit of an antique, but it did its job. Tests have been done fairly recently on vests like this. If I recall, four nine-millimeter rounds were fired from a distance of twenty-four feet, and the deepest penetration wasn't even halfway.'

'But closer up?'

He shook his head. 'It might knock you over, and it might bruise your skin, but penetrate? No way, Jose.'

'You're sure?'

'Look, you can buy any kind of surplus vest today, not that you would necessarily want to. There's nothing wrong with them. Remember, the original goal was to get a ninety-five-percent survival rate from getting hit with a .38 at a velocity of eight hundred feet per second.'

It seemed to be dawning on Dave that I was in the market for information more than anything else.

'Well,' I said, 'if I'm wearing that vest and someone fires the nine millimeter at me, as I described, how can I get a slug in the chest?'

'If you've got it on properly, if you've got the right size, and if there are no defects in the material — that's three ifs — you can't. Matter of fact, studies show that officers who *don't* wear vests are fourteen times more likely to risk fatal injury than those who do.'

'Thanks. I appreciate your time and patience.'

Dave tried to figure ways to lasso a sale as he followed me to the door.

'If you decide you want to buy, come back. We'll deal, especially in quantity.'

'I'll do just that.'

The last of the rush-hour traffic was trickling home. I picked up a cheeseburger and soft drink from a hamburger stand and ate on the drive back to Broad Ripple. There was a line of customers at Star Liquors, but Hurt wasn't behind the counter. A young man with his cap on backwards was ringing up the sales.

I went around the line. 'Excuse me. I'm looking for Mr Hurt.'

'He's off today.'

'Do you know where I can find him? I'm a friend.'

'Try the Jazz Joint down the street. If he's not there now he'll be there by dark.'

The Jazz Joint was a restaurant a block and a half away. It had a New Orleans motif featuring jazz combos playing indoors and outdoors on a deck under gondola lights. Broad Ripple was already starting to get crowded, and there was a line waiting to get in the place.

Hurt had a table by himself on a corner of the deck. He was eating a salad and tapping his fingers on the table. He wore a white suit with a blue shirt and white tie. He looked dignified and private, perhaps even lonely.

'Hello, Mr Hurt,' I said.

'You. You're here for the music?'

'I'm here for you. Mind if I sit down?'

'I do mind. I don't suppose that'll stop you. You're a pistol, Mr Ritter. You are a pistol.'

I sat down. The combo was playing improvised blues about twenty feet away. Hurt continued eating as if I weren't there.

I said, 'You told me you were arrested on a frame-up once. Mind telling me what happened?'

Hunt wiped his mouth with a linen napkin and took a long draught of his iced tea. He stared at me for a moment.

'Liquor licenses. I did an investigation. Found out some of them were being secretly funneled to the county chairman. Helluva story. Well, the prosecutor was a buddy of the chairman, and the prosecutor wanted to be governor. To make a long story short, they got some clerk to swear I'd bribed her to get information.' He took another sip of tea. 'Well, the paper reared up her hind legs. Went to war with the prosecutor. The voters are smarter than we give them credit for. They sent the prosecutor packing. The charge against me was thrown out. The rest of it was covered up. End of story.'

'How did you feel when you were arrested?'

'Angry. Humiliated. And, I guess I don't mind admitting, scared. You know why? When I sat down with our lawyer, he said, 'Look, you'd better understand one thing. There's a possibility you'll be convicted and sent to prison.' Well, sir, those are words to make you stand at attention, especially when you're innocent.'

We sat there for a minute listening to the music.

'I was arrested last night, Mr Hurt. Charged with possession of cocaine with intent to sell. The police planted the drugs.'

'I'm sorry. I didn't know.'

'And I don't mind telling you, I'm scared. It's a nice little set-up. At the minimum, I'm going to be disbarred. Do you want to know why? Because I kept asking questions about Griffo.'

Hurt's expression didn't change.

'How did they plant this cocaine?'

'I think through a woman I met, a dancer who's been working at Butch Tunney's place.'

If I expected Hurt to express shock, disgust, or sympathy, he didn't. He just made a low whistling noise and turned his head back and forth.

'You're quite a character, Mr Ritter. Found out what happens when you go up against certain people with power. So now you might be disbarred and have to go to work for a living. And the big shots will laugh through their noses, as they usually do.'

We listened to the laughter and chatter of the diners and the sweet rhythms of the music. I said nothing. I had made my pitch the best way I knew how.

Hurt's dinner arrived. It was a seafood platter with a side dish of au gratin potatoes. Hurt stared at his food.

'You know, Mr Ritter, to tell you the truth, I don't trust lawyers. They'll make up things to trick you. They'll make promises they won't keep. They'll say, 'Look, just tell me this and it'll never come back to you.' Next thing you know, you're being handed a subpoena.'

'All I can give you is my word. And tell you about this time last night, a police officer had a boot on my neck.'

The old reporter moved his food around with a fork.

'That woman you work with, she looks like my daughter. Funny thing about fathers. We raise our children and then there's really not much left to do. But, you know, we want our children to be happy and successful, very much so.' He raised an eyebrow. 'If I tell you a story, it's because I want to help someone's daughter. I will expect anonymity.'

'You have my pledge.'

Hurt grunted, a noise suggesting he had seen pledges of anonymity self-dissolve.

'Some years ago, a woman came to the paper with a problem. She was a policeman's wife. Her husband was abusing her. Beating her, terrorizing her. She said he was a mental case. Said he was drinking, depressed, bitter, suicidal. Said he'd sit around in the bedroom sucking on the barrel of his gun. Now, that was one of two problems. The second problem was this. She couldn't get the department to help her. Said they just rallied around her husband, wanted to protect him, and told her to be patient and understanding. While she was being patient and understanding, he would come home and knock her around, and threaten to kill her, and threaten to kill himself. The woman's name was Anna Griffo.'

Hurt stared at me. I was afraid to say anything, afraid he would stop.

'Well, I gave her a thorough debriefing. I told her I'd see what I could do. I realized she had to be totally desperate to come to the newspaper for help. I sent a note to the editor. I was busy on some story, I don't remember what. Anyway, the note got shuffled around for a while, maybe a couple of weeks. Then it came back to me, suggesting I put together some kind of story. So I called Mrs Griffo. She told me to forget it. She said her husband had agreed to counseling. She was still scared, and she begged me not to put anything in the paper. She made me promise to forget the whole thing. Couple of weeks later, her husband was shot to death.'

'Is that why you called Jackson's lawyer before the trial?'

'I thought it was information he should have. He never called me back.'

'Any idea why?'

'There could have been a dozen reasons. I remember this lawyer was the same lawyer who called me in Tunney's behalf, to threaten to sue me. Which was a crock, because the man obviously didn't have a clue about libel law. Maybe that was it. Maybe he thought I wanted to do a story on Jackson. Maybe he didn't like reporters. You tell me.'

'Do you remember anything else? Anything pertinent?'

'Pertinent? I don't know. She did say her husband was going to the Eastside Health Clinic. I remember that, because the clinic was federally funded, supposedly for low-income people.'

Hurt poked a fork into his food.

'I told you a story, and you're going to forget who it was that told you. That's that. I'll tell you this. I never could forget the image of a city police sergeant sitting in his bedroom with a .38 stuck in his mouth. Now, my food's getting cold. Why don't you leave me in peace?'

I wanted to hug Hurt, but I left without another word. I looked back to wave, and he didn't see me. He was busy consuming his dinner and trying not to let the past consume him.

In two minutes I was in my car. In fifteen I was racing northwest on the interstate. I looked at my watch. I'd missed Kit's six o'clock call, if she called, and it was now a quarter to eight.

The sun was dropping in a shower of orange and gold. The traffic on the interstate was thick, and began thinning as I left the capital city behind. I kept checking my watch. Kit was supposed to call at eight. What if she didn't? If she didn't call until ten, I'd still be nearly an hour away from the prison.

Kit's cell phone beeped at exactly eight.

'Kit? I'm on my way up there. See if you can get the governor's office to stop the execution. J.J. didn't deliberately murder Griffo.'

'What?' Kit shouted.

'It was a suicide by cop in reverse. Johnny Griffo wanted to die, and he made Jeremiah Jackson his executioner.'

24

The speed limit was sixty-five. I drove at exactly sixty-five. There was nothing I could do until I reached the prison. North of Lafayette I cut off on the state highway heading directly north to Michigan City. With full darkness the sky was filled with stars.

I was in a rural area when Kit called at ten.

'Where are you now, Sonny?'

'About forty-five minutes from the prison. Did you get the governor?'

'No. He's in Colorado. I talked to Larry Lynch. He said he'll try to find the governor, but he's hostile. Wants to know what proof we have.'

I almost spat into the phone. 'The hell with proof. We'll get the proof. The point right now is we're raising a new and compelling issue. They need to put the thing off. What difference does it make if they kill Jackson tonight or a week from tonight?'

Kit sounded frustrated. 'I explained that. Larry wants evidence this isn't some lawyer's trick, to use his words. Sonny, you know how this administration is. They just want to get this out of the way. What can you tell me?'

'I can tell you we'll produce evidence Griffo was depressed, possibly psychotic, and unquestionably suicidal. We'll grill the living shit out of everybody who worked with him. We will have proof. Make this point, Kit. We're not going to claim Jackson didn't shoot Griffo, just that the circumstances don't make it capital murder. We need a crack. If we don't come up with convincing evidence, well, hell, they can draw and quarter Jackson next week.'

'Let me see what I can do.'

Kit hung up.

I had been to the prison maybe a dozen times, never at night. With the perimeter bathed in security lights, the buildings appeared like a black-and-white movie against the horizon. Outside the main gate a dozen or so people, some carrying homemade signs, were walking back and forth, and two TV mobile units were parked by the guardhouse. As far as I could see, the protestors were all white people, most of them probably from local churches, with a few of the diehards who would picket even if Hitler were to be executed.

It took longer than usual to get through. I passed an extra security check. But there was plenty of time left, more than an hour, when two guards escorted me into the block building where executions were held. One guard explained there were two assembly rooms, one for those who wanted Jackson dead, one for his supporters.

I told the guard I needed to talk to Kit. He led me through a room with three people, probably members of Jackson's family or Mrs Jackson's church, through a door into a smaller room. Kit was talking on a wall phone, and waved her hand.

The room had a green metal desk and two green metal chairs. Another door had a window showing a corridor in front of another room that had a rectangular window covered with mesh. Behind the mesh I could see the backs of Mrs Jackson and her minister. They were talking to J.J. He wore a white shirt and pants and was smoking a cigarette. He looked calm and resigned.

The guard watched as I waited for Kit. When she hung up, she hugged me.

'Larry says he's unable to locate the governor. The warden won't delay without direct word from the governor. There's no time to get a judge.'

'Lynch's showing his true colors.'

'I agree. Talking to him is like talking to Pontius Pilate.'

'Where is the warden?'

'Next door. He's very reasonable, very

professional.' She looked at her watch. 'Everybody has to go in to the main assembly room at eleven-thirty. That's when they begin prepping J.J. The warden explained everything. Patient, I must say.'

'It takes thirty-five minutes to prep him?'

Kim nodded glumly. 'They give him ten ccs. of an antihistamine, to relax him.'

'Did you talk to Jackson?'

Kit looked through the window, across the corridor.

'I spent two hours with him. He seems . . . okay, I guess. Very creepy experience. He said to thank you. He sounds quite sincere. He'll get to say something before the procedure. He's going to apologize for killing Griffo.'

'Hell, he did Griffo a favor. And if that isn't the greatest irony I've ever heard, I'd like to know what is.'

We waited. I told Kit about my afternoon and evening. Fifteen minutes later, Warden Joseph Tanner came into the room. He was a broad-shouldered, mustachioed man of sixty, wearing a vested gray suit, who spoke in a whispery minister's voice and surprised me with his friendliness.

'You can have a few minutes to say goodbye,' he told Kit. 'Mr Ritter, too, if you want. We just gave him a mild sedative.'

'Will he be coherent?' I asked.

'Very much so. Five minutes prior to bringing him into the chamber, he'll receive a five-gram dose of sodium pentathal. That will have a major calming influence.'

'Isn't sodium pentathal one of the drugs you use to . . .'

'Yes, it is. It's the first of the three drugs. But a much larger dose.'

Tanner shook my hand. 'We're all professionals here. You've done your job the best you could, and now we'll do our job the best we can.'

The guard unlocked the door. Reverend Foster had just stepped out of the other room, his face drawn and somber, and he shook my hand.

'One at a time, and one minute only,' said Tanner.

Kit went in first. There was an expressionless guard standing in the corner and two others waiting outside. The door closed. Kit and Mrs Jackson hugged. Kit held Jackson's right hand with both of hers for four or five seconds. I couldn't read his lips. Her face blank, she came out, and I went in.

'Oh, Mr Ritter,' Mrs Jackson said, embracing me with resolution, weariness, and sadness. She wore a black dress suitable for a funeral and new black shoes.

J.J. held up a cigarette, let the guard light it

with a plastic lighter, and exhaled as he shook my hand.

'Guess it's my last,' he said. 'See, momma, I told you I'd quit.'

'Good luck to you, J.J.,' I said.

'Thank you, Mr Ritter,' he said in his smoky voice. 'Remember that promise you made me, about gold.'

'I'll do what I can.'

'Well . . . '

Mrs Jackson was hugging her son as I stepped out. Kit's face was pale, and she had tears in her eyes. I noticed the minister was holding her elbow. Mrs Jackson came out a moment later, her face wet from crying.

'This way,' the guard said.

Tanner was starting to go into the room.

'Warden,' I said, 'we need to be near a phone. Miss Lake is communicating with the governor's office.'

'I understand. Well, there's no phone available out there, but you have my assurances, if the governor's office calls, you'll be notified.'

Kit's voice snapped at him. 'No. I need to call the chief of staff. *Now.*'

'You certainly have that right,' Tanner said mildly. 'You can use the same phone. The rest of you . . . '

A guard went with Kit, and another guard

followed the rest of us to the waiting room. It was oddly quiet there. The family members gathered around Mrs Jackson for a sobbing account of her last meeting with J.J. Foster and I shuffled our feet. The next time I looked at my watch it was ten minutes to midnight.

Kit came in a minute later, followed by a guard.

'I explained everything,' she said. 'He claims the governor's in a meeting or something. But he promised to talk to him. I made him promise.'

'Hell, he's only got fourteen minutes.'

'I know that.'

Nothing happened. The room was utterly silent.

At midnight, the door opened.

'You can come in,' the guard said. 'We will not tolerate any outburst of any kind. Anything at all will result in immediate ejection. This way, please.'

The viewing room looked like a small theater. The first thing I noticed was how cold it was. There were two sections, each with about twenty unpadded chairs. People were filing in from another door, some of them police officers in uniform. I saw Mrs Griffo with two men holding each arm. Behind her the contingent included Dickie Buckley, wearing a brown suit, but not O'Hara or anyone else I recognized. That side of the room out-numbered ours by about three to one. I saw no one I recognized from the media.

The chairs faced a long rectangular window covered by dark drapes. The lighting was muted, like a funeral home. The walls were royal blue, the floor white linoleum with tiny flecks and scuff marks.

Kit and I sat in the second row, behind the Jacksons. I couldn't look to see who was on the other side. I glanced at my watch. It was midnight.

Kit lowered her head and brought her mouth near my shoulder. She started to whisper something, and stopped, unable to continue. Her hand took mine and held it tight. My mouth was dry, and I could feel my pulse quickening.

I knew Jackson already had been given two drugs, probably orally. The others would be injected through a saline IV — sodium pentathol, pancuronium bromide, then the real kicker, potassium chloride.

There was a murmur when the curtains were pulled. The death chamber seemed unusually bright. It looked like a veterinarian's operating room. We could see a second window inside, the control room where the

246

lethal injection apparatus was controlled.

Jackson lay on a gurney in his white uniform, like something a painter or dentist would wear, his arms by his sides and slightly splayed outward. It was like staring at a large-screen television of a medical show, only with an unspeakable, throat-tightening aura of medical murder in the making. I felt Kit brace herself. Her hand was sweaty.

There was a second murmur when the curtains suddenly closed.

It was the last thing anyone expected. I checked my watch. Three minutes after midnight. They were supposed to begin the injections in two minutes.

Everyone waited in tense silence. Kit looked at me with her eyebrows raised. Hands were being raised to check watches. The moment of execution passed, and still the curtains remained closed. Every minute seemed to include an extra allotment of seconds. With each passing minute there was more murmuring.

At ten minutes past the hour, Kit stood up. She went to the door next to the screened window and said something to the guard. The guard went inside. The murmuring increased.

Mrs Jackson turned to look at me, and whispered, 'Do you think . . . '

'Ma'am, I don't know what to think.'

'Maybe our prayers,' Foster said, without finishing the sentence.

The door opened. The guard said something to Kit. She signaled me with her finger.

We went through the door into a hallway. There was an open portal into the death chamber. We could see Jackson lying prone with a man in a suit and a uniformed guard bent over him.

Tanner came out of another room behind us.

'I'm sorry,' he said. 'We have a problem. We can't find a vein. It's never happened before.'

'What?' said Kit.

'Quite frankly, we can't place the needle. Very unusual. We can't start until then.'

Surprise and shock rose in Kit's voice. 'You mean to tell me the man has to lie there for who knows how long while you try to stick a needle in him? This is unconscionable.'

'I'm telling you this as a courtesy,' Tanner said in an even voice. 'I know it's hard on Jackson, but what am I to do?'

'What if the tranquilizers wear off?'

Tanner rubbed his hands together. 'We're doing the best we can. If you make a fuss, I'll have to send you to the assembly room. Please.'

It was twelve-twenty. We stood there, fifteen feet from Jackson, staring in disbelief.

Tanner went in to stand behind the man in the suit, glancing at his watch every few minutes. The whole macabre scene struck me as unreal. The man in the suit kept probing Jackson's arms, pinching the skin, and making muttered comments we couldn't hear. This went on for a few more minutes.

Suddenly, the man turned, said something inaudible, and turned Jackson's neck with his hand. He had a syringe and seemed to be trying to ram it into Jackson's neck. Kit held my arm and turned her head.

Finally the man turned to Tanner and said something. It was twelve thirty-one. Tanner nodded, waved his hand, and everyone started moving, everyone except Jackson. He managed to lift his head a few inches and turn, and for the first time could see us through the open door. His sweaty face was stamped with fear and frustration.

Tanner came around through the hall a minute later.

'I'm sorry. You'll have to go back out and sit down. I'm truly sorry.'

'What exactly is going on?' Kit asked in a raw voice.

'We simply can't place the needle. The doctor is going to try to insert an angio-catheter in Jackson's foot.'

I heard my own numbed voice. 'He's not

tranquilized any more.'

Tanner shook his head and gestured at the guard.

Everyone stared at us when we stepped into the viewing room. I didn't dare look at Mrs Griffo. I could see a uniformed officer talking in whispers to a guard. When we sat down, Mrs Jackson asked Kit what was going on. Kit shook her head.

The next fifteen minutes were almost painful. A kind of shock had set in. People were whispering in a chain-reaction of information. I knew lethal injection wasn't quite the humane process advocates claimed, but I didn't expect it could be bungled this much. All I could think of was a terrified man strapped to a gurney and wondering when he was going to die.

The curtains didn't open again. Everyone sat mutely in their chairs, like mourners at a funeral home staring at a closed casket, uncertain whether it would be occupied when the lid was lifted.

At exactly twelve fifty-four, the door opened, and the warden came out.

He held out his hands palms up.

'Ladies and gentlemen,' Tanner said, 'by order of the governor, this execution has been postponed until next week.'

25

I thought the warden's announcement might produce cries of outrage. Instead, like a church congregation breaking up after some powerful sermon, people stood and adjusted their clothing and began filing out quietly. Probably everyone expected something like this after the long delay. Maybe they were in shock that the evening had unfolded exactly the opposite of the way it should have.

Mrs Griffo, flanked by two police officers, had a brief, animated conversation with Tanner before turning and walking out of the room, eyes staring straight ahead. Her face looked like it had been rubbed with chalk. Buckley walked behind her, his eyes void of feeling but his mouth twisted.

Mrs Jackson, shaking her head as if witness to a miracle, embraced Kit while Foster pumped my hand.

'I don't know what you did,' the minister said, 'but I can assure you, you didn't do it by yourselves.' He lifted his face upward, his eyes ablaze in the certainty of some celestial connection. 'You had the kind of help that never disappoints.'

'Praise the Lord,' Mrs Jackson said.

'I'm afraid this is just one in a series of battles,' I told Foster. 'We won this one, somehow, and might lose the next.'

Mrs Jackson patted me on the shoulder. 'Give yourself some credit, young man. And this lady, too,' she added, squeezing Kit.

'Do you think we'll be able to see J.J.?' Foster asked.

'I doubt it,' said Kit. 'Maybe tomorrow, or the day after.'

'Does this mean . . . you know, that they won't be able to execute J.J.?'

'The honest answer is, I don't know,' Kit told him. 'I'm guardedly optimistic.'

Mrs Jackson's jubilant laughter shook her body. 'Well, we don't need the Supreme *Court*. We've got the Supreme *Being*.'

'Will you be riding back with us, Miss Lake?' Foster inquired.

'No, I'll ride with Mr Ritter. I know we're all exhausted and emotionally spent. Please, drive carefully.'

Foster took Mrs Jackson's hand. 'We will, young lady. We surely will.'

'I'll be in touch in a few days,' Kit promised.

'Thank you again, thank you again,' said Mrs Jackson.

Tanner was about to return to the death

chamber. I intercepted.

'Warden, what time did the governor call?'

Tanner cleared his throat. 'Well, he called at twelve forty-eight.'

'Did you have the catheter in?'

'Yes, just about.'

'In other words, if he'd called a couple minutes later, Jackson would be dead.'

'Realistically, yes.'

'And if you'd been able to insert the needle as you planned to, Jackson would be dead.'

'Correct again. Understand, however, that the problems with inserting the syringe system were one of the reasons, I would say the main reason, why the governor decided to postpone the procedure. There'll be a full review. Steps will be taken. The manual doesn't anticipate this problem.'

Kit interposed herself. 'Thank you for your courtesy, warden. One question. In view of tonight's gruesome experience, do you support capital punishment?' She smiled wickedly. 'You don't have to answer. Good-night.'

It seemed as if we'd been in the building all night. Outside, the muggy air felt surprisingly refreshing. Kit squeezed my hand, signaling relief at leaving the state's house of death.

'What a night.'

'You said it.'

'You did it, Sonny. Somehow, you did it. I'm proud of you.'

'And I'm proud of you.'

We inhaled the night air, feeling proud of each other.

'Do you think the governor's office delayed calling on purpose?' Kit asked as we walked to the car.

'I wouldn't put it past them. They must have got a shock if they called expecting to hear that Jackson was dead.'

'I think I hate politics.'

'Good old Larry showed his true colors, just as I knew he would.'

'Go ahead and say I told you so.'

'I'm too tired to gloat.'

'Well, it was a dirty trick. In a way, it was tantamount to attempted murder.'

'Larry is the state. The state doesn't murder. The state terminates in the name of justice.'

'You can write your editorial on the way back to Indianapolis.'

For half an hour neither of us said anything as we drove south on the state highway under the star-filled sky. Finally Kit sighed, and said, 'Mrs Griffo knew. She had to know.'

'I feel sorry for her. In her shoes, maybe I would have done the same thing.'

'When did you begin to figure it out?'

'This morning. The proverbial lightbulb went off when I tried to answer your question, how Griffo could have been shot in the chest. I had no idea, until a jail deputy happened to mention Houdini.'

'Houdini?'

'When I was a kid, I bought a book about Houdini. The book described how he did most of his tricks. It had illustrations showing his gimmicks, trap doors and the like. I was crushed. I didn't want to know this stuff. I liked the idea of magic.'

'And?'

'And I remembered Houdini talked about one of his keys, that you see what you see and you don't see what you can't see. You see the outside of the box, but not the special compartment inside. That's what I realized about the videotape. We didn't see what we couldn't see.'

'And we could see Griffo's back, but not his hands.'

'Exactly. You asked how Griffo could get shot in the chest through a bulletproof vest. The answer is, he couldn't. Unless he ripped open the Velcro himself. Who would do something like that? A man who wanted to die.'

'In effect, suicide.'

'In effect and in fact. That's why he was

first in. That's why he yelled, 'You're a dead man,' to give Jackson motive to shoot rather than surrender. If it didn't happen that day, it would happen another day. The man had a death wish. I feel sorry for him. I wish I knew what turned him.'

'Maybe he was just sick of being the wrong kind of cop, or not being the kind of policeman he wanted to be when he came back from Vietnam.'

'Or maybe Vietnam did something to him. Post traumatic stress disorder, for instance.'

'So when Buckley realized what happened, he closed the vest.'

'We'll never get Buckley to admit it.'

Kit was quiet for a half-hour before she said, 'I'll be damned if I'm going to let them get away with it.'

'Let who get away with what?'

'The state. Larry. Buckley. O'Hara. All of them. It's not right. We'll petition for a new trial.'

'The Supreme Court won't do anything without hard evidence.'

'We'll get hard evidence. You'll get hard evidence. You must have more leads.'

'One. The Eastside Health Clinic.'

'Good. You can't finish without a place to start.'

She was quiet for a few minutes. Then, 'I

still can't believe it. I expected to be driving home after watching a man die.'

'You may yet have the experience.'

'Your father will be pleased, anyway.'

'He will?'

'More than you know.'

'Why do you think my dad will be so pleased?'

'He had a visitor the other day. Sheldon Coover. He's not just the chairman of Penrod Pharmaceuticals. He's also the head of a committee of businessmen who help out the widows of police officers. In so many very polite words, Mr Coover suggested he didn't care for his law firm representing a cop killer. Your father told him, in so many very polite words, to drop dead.'

'My dad did? Good for him.'

We rode in numb silence for nearly an hour. I could almost see Kit's brain cranking away. Then she said, 'Don't look so glum.'

'Do I look glum? Sorry. I was just thinking. Griffo used Jackson to commit suicide, and Jackson still could be executed, and I'm probably going to be disbarred and sent to prison. Other than that, I don't have anything to be glum about. What kind of word is glum, anyway? It sounds like something you use to clean your hubcaps.'

'Did I ever tell you you're a male chauvinist pig?'

'I studied at the feet of Dr Chauvin himself. If it'll make you feel better, you can tell me again.'

'You're a male chauvinist pig.'

I forced a toothy smile. 'Thanks, I needed that. I was afraid my fellow pigs might demote me.'

'Actually, I'm serious. You know what your problem is? You're a good lawyer. You've got a good heart. You believe in the law, and you work hard for your clients. You don't give up.'

'I can't wait 'til you get to the nice stuff.'

'But you want to do everything yourself. You want to take on the world with no help from anyone. It's all by your lonesome against everybody. When those phony klansmen were chasing us the other night, you should have seen your face. You were scared as hell, and you were practically ecstatic. You were on a testosterone high. You were rescuing poor little Kit from the bad guys, as if that's what you were born to do.'

'Well, *excuse me*. Next time we can light the cross and have a wienie roast.'

'I'm saying this for a reason. How about giving me a chance to save your bacon? Can you put aside the jokes and trust me completely?'

'You want to save the bacon of a male chauvinist pig? Be my guest. Exactly how do you plan to do this?'

'I have an idea, that's all. Let me run with it. For just once, put your trust in a woman. Can you do that?'

'On one condition.'

'Name it.'

'If it doesn't work, you'll visit me in prison.'

Kit smiled in a conspiratorial way. 'You've got a deal.'

26

Exhaustion nudged me into sleep as soon as I collapsed into bed in the middle of the night. Exhilaration jolted me awake an hour later. By all rights, I should have slept all day. Instead, I felt as if I could run a marathon carrying anvils under each arm. The events of the last twenty-four hours churned through my head.

While coffee brewed, I put on a Schubert string quartet and soaked in a deliciously hot tub for half an hour. Never had I heard more beautiful music. I slipped on khakis and a pullover shirt and took the coffee to the front porch. The *Chronicle* hadn't arrived yet. Dawn was less than an hour away.

I walked around the yard enjoying the sweet sultriness of the summer air and the squishing of dewy grass on my bare feet. I looked at the fading lavender blossoms of the rose of Sharon bush and studied the pattern of a spider's web translucent in the light of the moon. I saw an old yellow tomcat skulking along the back fence on his return from night patrol, and watched two startled cardinals dart out of the crabapple tree and disappear, bat-like, against the sky.

Life was precious, and I was glad to be alive. I wondered what J.J. Jackson would feel when he opened his eyes. I realized, too, that John Griffo deserved to be alive, and until I knew why he wasn't, I had unfinished business.

Inside I poured more coffee and turned on the TV. The all-night cable station played yesterday's news, including a brief out-of-date story about J.J.'s impending execution. I flipped channels and finally settled on a puffy evangelist guaranteeing miracles for money.

When the phone rang, I knew it was Kit before I heard her voice.

'You're not going to guess what I just did,' she said. 'At four o'clock in the morning I went to the Waffle House and had the biggest breakfast I've had in years. Sonny, I pigged out! I ate everything except the plate.'

'You used to do that back in school, remember? After a night of drinking we'd go to White Castle and eat a bag of sliders. We had cast-iron stomachs.'

'Don't mention sliders,' Kit groaned. 'Anyway, I've been up half the night. I feel like I'm on an amphetamine high. Last night started out as a nightmare and ended up as, I don't know, a daydream.'

'I have the same feeling. I don't want to

lose the momentum. As soon as the sun comes out, I'm going to play detective.'

'Not without me. I'm going to the office. You can pick me up there.'

'Okay. Maybe we'd be better wait until everybody else gets up. How does nine sound?'

'I'll be out front.'

Kit's talk about food reminded me how hungry I was. I put on my running outfit and worked up a sweat doing half of my usual routine. When I returned home I took a quick shower, dressed in a suit, and drove to the nearest Waffle House. I had a Belgian waffle soaked in a buttery pool of syrup, side orders of sausage, bacon, and hash browns, two big glasses of orange juice, and more coffee. It was the worst breakfast I'd had in years. It was delicious.

At five minutes past nine I picked up Kit in front of the AUL building. She wore a shapely pearl-gray linen dress and had her hair pinned in a bun. She looked bright and pinkishly healthy.

'I have a very important conference at two,' she said. 'I'm yours 'til then. Where to?'

'The Eastside Health Clinic.'

'Where is it?'

'It isn't.'

'It isn't what?'

'It isn't there.'

I remembered the clinic had closed two or three years ago due to cutbacks in the federal budget. I hoped there would be other offices to point us in the right direction. As soon as I turned off Pleasant Run Parkway, into a transition area between an old neighborhood and a lengthy stretch of strip malls and mostly empty buildings, I prepared for disappointment. The former home of the clinic was abandoned.

It was a collection of three sooty red brick buildings, each two stories, surrounded by a waist-high wire fence. Weeds grew along the curb and all the way up the sidewalk to the front entrance. I parked out front.

'It's been empty for years,' Kit said.

'Yeah. I'll be right back.'

I left the car running and stepped into the muggy morning heat. The front gate had a chain and padlock, and a black-and-white sign the size of a license plate. The sign was a notice from the General Services Administration telling people to stay out. There was an 800 number to call for inquiries.

The drone of a motor came from around the corner. I walked towards the back to identify the source. It came from a riding mower puttering across the grass. The operator, a shirtless man who looked to be about sixty, saw me and waved. He turned off the engine as I approached.

He was a bulky fellow with more hair on his back than his jowly, bulldog head.

'Good morning,' I said. 'I wonder if you can tell me how I can get in touch with the people who ran the clinic. I'm looking for records.'

His eyebrows were two brown caterpillars that immediately wiggled upward. He stepped off the mower.

'Well, I'll be damned. It sure as hell took you long enough. I'm Denny Parr. You can knock me over with a feather.'

'Sonny Ritter,' I said as we shook hands. 'I think you're expecting someone else. I'm an attorney.'

'Hell, I thought you were with the government. No one else'd give a wet fart about this place. I'm going to guess the GSA hired you. Independent contractor, like me.'

'I don't represent the GSA, Mr Parr. Matter of fact, I'd like to talk to someone from the GSA.'

'So would I.' He rubbed his whiskered chin. 'Well, if you're not from the government, how'd you know about the records?'

'What records?'

'The clinic records. That's what you want, isn't it?'

'Yes, but the clinic's closed.'

Parr wiped his face with a red bandana. 'Oh, now I get it.' He extracted a crumpled pack of Camels from his pocket and lit one with a kitchen match. 'They closed the place down. Three years ago. Soon as the government money disappeared, so did everyone else. Me, I'm the caretaker. I mow the lawn and pick up the litter, and they mail me a check every quarter. Nice check. I'm not complaining about that.'

'What are you complaining about?'

'After they closed the place, I found six file cabinets. Six! Full of records, personal and private stuff. I called the GSA. They didn't do squat. So I wrote a letter. Nothing. So I called the TV stations. Channel Six came out. They did a story. I was on TV. Some woman from the GSA said. 'Yeah, we're sorry, we'll take care of it.' Want to know what happened?'

'Nothing?'

Parr bobbed his head. 'Nothing. Nobody really gives a shit.'

'I do. What happened to those cabinets?'

'I've got 'em. I'm going to sell them for salvage. Pay for my troubles. I'll burn the papers first. What's your interest?'

'It's a confidential matter involving an important client. I'll probably end up subpoenaing the records, but I'd like to look at them first.'

'No problem. See that garage?' He pointed over the fence to the nearest home. It was a one-story brick house with a gravel driveway. The white garage had two bays and looked like it needed to be painted. 'Drive on over. I'll meet you.'

I grinned at Kit when I got in the car.

'Don't say a word. The clinic records may be in the caretaker's garage. Let me do the talking.'

'You don't think . . . '

'We'll know in a few minutes.'

Parr took a shortcut around the fence and walked up as we got out of the car. When he saw Kit, his stomach went in as his chest came out.

'This is Mr Parr,' I said. 'This is my associate, Kit Lake.'

Parr managed to say hello without exhaling.

'There they are.' He pointed to the bay on the left. 'Holler if you need anything. I've got to finish my mowing.'

The interior smelled of musty wood, the dirt floor, and the black 1952 Chevrolet, partly restored sitting tireless on concrete blocks. It was as much an attic as a garage, with junk piled everywhere. The cabinets lined the right wall. All of them were gunmetal gray except one, the tallest with

266

four drawers, that had been painted white.

'You start here,' I told Kit. 'I'll start at the other end.'

Most of the drawers had no labels. The second cabinet I looked at had hand cut white cards in tiny slots. All of them said PATIENTS/CLIENTS.

'Kit,' I said. I couldn't believe our luck.

Kit leaned over me as my hand raced through the tabs of brown folders, each bearing a typed name, all of them in alphabetical order.

'There,' Kit said.

I pulled the folder out, holding my breath as I read the name GRIFFO, JOHN. It was thin — very thin.

'Let me see,' Kit pressed.

Inside was a single yellow sheet, a printed form with questions answered in scribbled ink. It was an application for services, containing the same kind of basic information about Griffo I saw in his personnel file.

'Shit,' I said.

'Maybe the rest is misfiled. Let's check the other drawers.'

As we went through drawer after drawer and folder after folder, the thrill fizzled away. There were no medical records of any kind.

The air in the garage was stifling. When I stepped outside, Parr waved from his riding mower. I waved back.

Kit came out into the sun. 'What now, Sherlock?'

'Give me a minute. I'm thinking.'

'Well, for a minute I thought the whole thing had just landed in our laps. Everything you wanted to know about Johnny Griffo and were afraid to ask.'

'I know.'

Kit held the yellow sheet in front of her. 'At least it proves Griffo came here for treatment. Look at the date. Seven weeks before the shooting.'

'I noticed.'

'We'll find the doctor. We'll find the records. We should have plenty to get a new trial.'

I could feel a smile crossing over my face. 'Maybe we won't have to.'

'Won't have to what?'

'We've got Griffo's official file from the clinic, don't we?'

'Sure, but it's empty.'

'You know that. I know that. Anna Griffo doesn't.'

27

The house surprised me. I expected something larger, maybe one of the fancier homes scattered throughout the area known as Irvington, a place with French windows and a tiled roof and a privacy fence covered with ivy. Certainly a swimming pool.

Real estate brochures would describe the Griffo residence as a 'charmer.' It was single story and box-like, probably with no more than two bedrooms. An arrangement of stone and red brick covered the exterior. It looked like most of the surrounding homes, except the front porch had been enclosed with storm windows and the small front lawn showed some imagination in the landscaping. The evergreen bushes had been pruned to shape, and the flower bed at the base of the porch offered a mixture of colors, dominated at both ends by swarms of black-eyed Susans.

Most of the lawns in the neighborhood were parched. This one was green and wet. An oscillating sprinkler tossed shiny beads in a lazy circular pattern. People tend to turn off their sprinklers when they go away. This suggested Anna Griffo was at home. Whether she would answer the door was another matter.

I parked out front. I grabbed some papers from the rear seat and tucked them inside the clinic folder to make it appear thicker. I turned the folder outward, to make sure the name on the tab was visible.

Kit nodded as she opened the door. There was no point in hatching a game plan.

From the walkway I could see the white-frame garage at the end of the driveway. Both bay doors were closed. Someone had been digging along the side of the house with a hand trowel. The tool lay on the ground next to a large green watering can. Four rose bushes had been trimmed and the brown clippings left in a pile.

At the door I knocked hard enough to alert the neighbors, if they weren't already alert.

Kit smiled and said without moving her lips, 'She won't even come to the door.'

The inner door opened. Anna Griffo came out and unlatched the porch door, pulling it back about eighteen inches.

'Mrs Griffo . . . ' I started to say.

'Come in,' she said in a low, nearly toneless voice. 'I've been expecting you.'

I caught Kit's look, and let her go first.

The porch had an earthy smell, probably from an array of potted plants and flowers lined along the ledge. There was an old-fashioned two-seat swing with the chain painted green. From below a Siamese cat stuck out its head and yawned.

We passed through wordlessly. I didn't know what to say. I assumed Mrs Griffo wanted to unleash an indignant sermon about lawyers gumming up the machinery of justice.

Walking past her, I was surprised at how short she was. With bare feet she stood maybe five feet, and had thin arms and wrists. She wore a man's T-shirt and cut-off jeans. Her hair was plain, merely brushed. Her face had been freckled by the sun. Dirt discolored her fingers and nails.

'You can sit there,' she said, her voice only ashes where fire had once burned.

She pointed to a sturdy Colonial couch. Most of the furniture in the living room looked expensive but old. With the drapes drawn, the room had a shadowy, cloistered feeling. There was an old scuffed-up piano in one corner. The fireplace had been darkened by soot. The mantel had a dozen pictures in frames of different shapes and sizes. As I sat down, I realized John Griffo wasn't in any of the photos. In fact, the room had nothing to suggest his former presence.

Mrs Griffo stood in front of us, gently

wringing her hands. Her face was blank and her eyes were dark and heavy. The way she stood and moved suggested tension seeking release, as if she might suddenly start screaming at us.

Instead, to my surprise, or perhaps shock, she said, 'I'm willing to cooperate to end this thing. Exactly what is it you want?'

Kit looked at me. I looked at Kit. Nervously, I placed the folder on my lap.

'A new trial for Jackson,' I said.

'I won't stand in the way. What else?'

'The truth,' Kit said.

The words hung in the air.

Mrs Griffo turned. She picked up a cloth purse from a maple end table and extracted a pack of cigarettes. She lit one with a lighter, turned, and sat on the edge of a rocker. She took a deep drag, and exhaled.

'If I tell you what you want to know, the so-called truth, I want your word, both of you. It stays here.'

'Anything you tell us will remain confidential,' Kit said, 'with one disclaimer. It can't be confidential if we already know it. Frankly, we know quite a bit.'

'We've been to the health clinic,' I said. 'We found your husband's records.'

Mrs Griffo almost snorted. 'Of all the mistakes, *that* was one of the biggest.'

'I'm sorry,' said Kit. 'I know this has been an eight-year ordeal.'

Mrs Griffo took a deep drag. 'Longer than eight years. This isn't easy for me. About my confidentiality, you didn't really promise.'

'What I can tell you is this,' I said. 'We don't want to hurt or embarrass you. You said you want to end this thing. That's all we want. We don't believe Jackson deserves to be executed.'

She crushed the cigarette in a blue ashtray. The only noise in the house was a faint hum that I finally identified as the water pump in the basement.

Her voice was flat and unemphatic.

'Last night . . . I thought, I expected, I don't know, some *satisfaction*. The word you hear all the time is closure. I thought the man would be put to sleep and not wake up, and that would end everything. I didn't expect the whole thing to be so . . . repulsive. The idea of sitting there watching the state kill him, his mother, all those people. It wasn't like I thought it would be. I wanted to walk out. And when I did, I realized I was glad — relieved — that they didn't execute him. I thought, well, put him in a cage, but don't kill him and ask me to watch. It made me feel . . . little.'

I said, 'You believe Jackson murdered your

husband. We believe your husband helped him.' I couldn't force myself to use the word suicide.

'Johnny never trusted lawyers,' she said. 'And now I have no choice. I said I want to end this. But it has to be done without dragging everyone through the mud. Anyway, it's all so . . . old.'

'You must have loved your husband very much,' Kit said.

Mrs Griffo simply shrugged. She looked like a person who no longer had the strength to hold her shoulders up.

'Johnny was a good cop. Maybe not perfect, but good. He believed in what he did. He wanted to help people. Then, over the years, things changed. He didn't think the public cared. He thought the system was corrupt. A lot of officers were getting something on the side. So Johnny did, too. Then, when he made detective, he got partnered with Dickie. That's when things really changed. Dickie changed him. He became more like Dickie. Dickie's greedy, and he has a cruel streak. You have to realize how much time they spent together. It was like they were married. Like brothers, anyway.'

She reached for another cigarette but didn't light it immediately.

'Then he was drinking more. Moodier. We didn't get along like we used to. I know he had women on the side. He was living high. I mean, sometimes he wouldn't come home. When I tried to talk to him, he exploded. Then he hit me once.' She touched her cheek with her fingers. 'It's hard to explain. It was like he was on a train and couldn't get off. Didn't want to get off. One night, I told him I wanted a divorce. He beat me. Beat me pretty bad. See, I think Johnny loved me, but I reminded him of how much he'd changed. Try to understand, this happened over many years.'

'We do understand,' Kit said, saying what Mrs Griffo needed to hear.

'Finally, everything took its toll. The hours, the drinking, the I-don't-know-what. Johnny had trouble sleeping. He had to take pills. He became very depressed. When I tried to talk to him, he'd explode. I went to the department chaplain. The chaplain talked to Johnny. Things were better. For a few months, things were better. Then they went back to the way they were. Sometimes, when he was really bad, he talked about how he hated the world for being what it is.'

'You must have sought further counseling,' Kit said. 'But you said the health clinic was a mistake.'

'I'll get to that. Yes, I sought help. I went to John's superiors. They promised to talk to him. They said everything would be all right. They told me not to make waves. Later, I realized they only had one concern. They wanted to protect Johnny. He was one of them, such a great guy, a sergeant, a detective sergeant, the great Johnny Griffo. Would they ask him to get help? Sure. Would they order him to get help? Never. Somehow, they assumed Johnny would pull himself out of the thing. You know, a few weeks' vacation, some R and R, help with his cases, that sort of thing.'

She lit the cigarette and coughed.

'So I went to Dickie. He was the only one who could help. I asked him to come over when Johnny wouldn't know. He was here, in this room. That night . . . that night . . . Dickie, he, well, there's no way to say it politely, he forced himself on me. He got his . . . satisfaction. When I told Johnny, he exploded. But not at Dickie. At me. It had to be me. I'd seduced Dickie. Dickie would never go behind Johnny's back. Of course that's what Dickie said, too. No, I was a lonely, horny housewife, that's what. He started beating me. I filed for divorce.'

'Why did you withdraw the petition?' I asked.

'The department. Johnny's friends. Suddenly everybody cared. They wanted him to get counseling. They wanted to set everything right again. They didn't want to make waves, have any kind of scandal. Johnny promised to get help. Arrangements were made for the clinic. Almost immediately, things were better. I withdrew the divorce. I felt pressured, but, I'll have to admit, I *wanted* things to get better. I didn't want it to end like that.'

'It must have been a terrible ordeal,' Kit said.

'Instead of getting better, it got worse. See, when my husband went in for counseling, he began to realize Dickie lied to him, and that I hadn't. He began to face up to the fact that his beloved partner had raped his wife. It was just too much for him. In some ways he got better, in some ways worse. He had these fits of depression. He started talking about suicide again. He was so bitter. He was confused and bitter. And yet, there wasn't anything I could do.'

There was silence for a moment. She had compressed years of a relationship into a five-minute summary, and she was groping to find some way to make certain we understood.

'What did you do?' I asked.

'Talked to Johnny. Talked to his superiors. I even talked to the deputy chief. They were 'keeping an eye' on things. Let the counseling work, they said. Johnny was up for lieutenant. They didn't say so directly, but they were worried about two things. First, Johnny's pension. A few years more and he could retire. But they were worried about scandal, too. If John got in trouble, he could talk about Dickie. About other things. He knew a lot.'

Kit said, 'On the day your husband was killed . . . '

'Yes, I more or less knew what happened. He'd talked about it often enough. Sometimes, I thought what he wanted to do was get into a situation, maybe cause a situation, where. Dickie was jeopardized, too. He loved Dickie, but he hated him. Hated him for betraying him.'

'You should have said something,' Kit said. 'Why didn't you?'

Mrs Griffo exhaled in a weary way. The cigarette had burned down and out, and she dropped the butt into the ashtray.

'Can't you guess? Can't you see? John Griffo died in the line of duty. That's what everybody knew and wanted. They didn't want to know he was having mental problems aggravated because of his partner. You have to understand, when Johnny was having his troubles, the department rallied around him, formed a circle to protect him. And when he died, they rallied around him again, only this time they brought me into the circle. I was the brave widow. I didn't care, to be honest. I really didn't. Jackson's just a criminal, and he did shoot my husband.'

Kit cleared her throat. 'Mrs Griffo, what changed your mind? What happened last night?'

A hiss came out. 'No. Yes, but more than just the experience. It was Dickie, the son of a bitch. The truth is, I haven't talked to him since the night he was here. I wouldn't talk to him at the funeral. I haven't seen him since. Then, last night, he's sitting next to me, like my protector. The hypocrite. I hate the man. I won't participate in this charade any longer.'

'I understand,' Kit said. 'I think I understand.'

It was done. We all knew it. There were no more secrets. I felt sorry for Anna Griffo. No one should be subjected to what she underwent.

I realized how lonely this house was now.

'Well,' she said, 'can you tell me what's going to happen?'

'We'll petition for a new trial,' Kit said. 'We'll be granted a new trial. The prosecutor, however, almost certainly will offer a deal.

Jackson will plead guilty. What will happen after that I'm not sure.'

'Closure,' Mrs Griffo said.

'None of this will have to come out,' Kit said.

'Thank you.'

Kit stood. 'We'll be in touch, probably in the next few days. Thank you for your time. Thank you for your candor.'

Mrs Griffo led us to the door. Expressions rather than words said goodbye.

As we got into the car, Kit said, 'I feel so sorry for her, I almost cried.'

'She's right about one thing. Buckley's a son of a bitch. And I'll bet Johnny was hoping J. J. Jackson would take him out, too. We'll never know.'

'I wish there was something we could do about him.'

'There isn't. Look at it this way. Now J. J. won't be executed. We've saved him. Now we just have to save me. Or have you save me.'

Kit gave me a funny look. 'I'm working on it.'

28

The phone woke me up at ten o'clock in the morning.

'I want you to come down here for a meeting at two,' Kit said. 'Several conditions. First, you say nothing. Second, no faces and no gestures. Third, absolutely nothing from you until the other party is gone. Agreed?'

'Who's the other party?'

'Never mind. Trust me. Yes or no?'

'Yes.'

At five to two I was in the reception area at Ritter Ritter Talmadge & Stokely, freshly barbered, dressed in my William Rehnquist suit used only on special occasions, and prepared to Super Glue my lips in order to comply with Kit's directives. I was also mad with curiosity. But it was Kit's game, and I had agreed to play by her rules.

'Hi,' I told the receptionist. 'I have an appointment with Katherine Lake.'

'Yes, she and the other gentleman just went in the main conference room. Go right in.'

I was so anxious I had to be careful not to pull the door off the hinges. The main conference room had a huge walnut table surrounded by leather chairs and a huge window with a beautiful view of downtown. There were probably twenty chairs, and only two were occupied.

Kit had one. Captain Milton O'Hara had the other.

'Come in and sit down, Sonny,' Kit said. 'We're just getting started. You know Captain O'Hara.'

In compliance with our agreement, I nodded to acknowledge O'Hara's presence. The captain was in uniform, his white shirt freshly ironed, his badged hat on the table, and nervous perplexity on his face.

'You said it was urgent and confidential,' he said to Kit. 'I'm here to listen.'

Kit lifted the briefcase on the floor next to her and unsnapped the top. She brought out a sheaf of papers and slid them over to O'Hara.

'These are copies for you, captain. You might want to glance through them before I say what I have to say.'

O'Hara picked up the stack gingerly, as if he didn't want to leave his fingerprints.

'Copies of what? If there's some . . . '

Kit's voice went up a notch, to a tone she saved for grilling reluctant witnesses.

'These are FBI memos, what they call 302s. There are thirty-two of them. They outline a rather shocking pattern of corruption in city hall and the police department. They detail names, dates, times, and places. They have direct information and corroborative information. Please, take a minute to look at the names.'

O'Hara's face went through a rainbow of colors, with emphasis on red. His eyes darted along the pages. Pro that he was, his voice didn't change.

'Assuming these are what you say they are, why give them to me?'

'Because you can prevent the biggest corruption scandal in the city's history,' Kit said.

O'Hara coughed, as if he suddenly had a furball in his throat. His face darkened in the realization that he had walked into a kind of trap. I could see enough of the pages to recognize the FBI reports Phil Curry gave me.

'And just how the hell can I do that?' said O'Hara, trying to sound authoritative and huffy.

'Simple,' said Kit. 'You will arrange for the department to dismiss the charges against Mr Ritter. You will arrange for the department to issue an apologetic press release completely and emphatically exonerating Mr Ritter. If you wish, you can have the department express shock that one of its informants would plant drugs in a lawyer's home, and perhaps announce new safeguards to prevent any recurrence. That's up to you.'

The silence that followed was so threatening I thought it might use up all the oxygen in the room. Captain O'Hara was doing some rapid-transit thinking.

After thirty or forty seconds, he tapped his fingers on the table and said, 'Assuming I could arrange such a thing, which I certainly can't, why would I?'

Kit had that sweet smile Delilah must have had when she slipped the scissors into Samson's curly locks.

'I don't suppose you know the name Richard Bleeker. Mr Ritter and I went to law school with Mr Bleeker. Mr Ritter, I think, will agree with me that Mr Bleeker certainly was the toughest S.O.B. in our class. Mr Bleeker has gone on to better things. He's the attorney in charge of the Department of Justice organized crime strike force in Chicago. If you don't do what I suggest, and do it by six o'clock tomorrow afternoon, at six-oh-one I will be on the phone arranging to get these memos into the hands of Mr Bleeker. Now, captain, I can assure you he would feel it his duty to turn the might of the strike force in the direction of a major police department gone astray.'

O'Hara started to say something. Kit held up her hand.

'One further point. As you know, the federal government prefers to use the Hobbs Act and RICO statute in corruption cases. You may not know, and I think you should, that RICO has a ten-year statute of limitations. And a police department in a case like this could be branded as a continuing enterprise. You may want to bear this in mind when you examine the reports.'

'Look . . . ' O'Hara started to say.

'No, you look,' Kit fired back. 'You take the memos and you look at the names, and you do what you have to do. Our meeting is over. There's nothing further to say. Except perhaps only that Mr Ritter will make himself available to sign a release agreeing not to sue the police department. That's all. Good day.'

I'm not sure who was more astonished. O'Hara stared at me like a man who had just found his head instead of the ball rolling down a bowling lane. I was so busy trying not to cheer, I thought I would burst.

O'Hara grabbed the papers and stood up. He took extra care putting his hat on. Then he looked at me in a strange way, as if I had somehow violated a masculine compact by letting a woman get the best of him.

Without another word, he walked out, leaving the door open.

Kit released a sigh big enough to inflate a raft, and grinned mischievously. 'How'd I do?'

'Kit . . . Kit . . . you were marvelous. Do you really think O'Hara will do what you want him to do?'

'Oh, you need to reread the memos. Look at the names. The mayor's office, the chief's office. Two judges. My goodness, certain people will move mountains to make this go away.'

'But the prosecutor's office . . . '

The mischievous smile went from the mouth to her eyes.

'I met yesterday afternoon with Terry Moss. I informed Mr Moss that we have substantial reason to believe a police informant planted drugs in your house at the behest of the police, which, of course, is a crime in itself. I made it clear to Mr Moss that having been given information about a crime, he as an officer of the court has a duty to investigate. I suggested that an interrogation of the informant might easily lead to a different story. I pointed out that the informant could be linked to a certain organized crime figure, who in turn could be linked to a certain hero police officer and his

286

partner, said partner presently working for said organized crime figure. I also suggested that if this information came out from another quarter, it could be highly embarrassing to the prosecutor's office, but, on the other hand, if he turned it up himself, it would reflect favorably on the office. I believe Mr Moss got the message.'

She caught her breath.

'Just to make sure, I gave Moss a set of the memos.' Kit all but twinkled. 'By the way, regardless of what O'Hara does, and how soon, a set also will reach the editor of the *Chronicle*. Anonymously, of course.'

I was close to speechless.

'Kit, you . . . '

'Yes, Mr Ritter?'

'Baby,' I said in my best Ralph Kramden voice, 'you're the greatest.'

Shortly after nine o'clock in the morning, the telephone rang in my office. At ten o'clock, a young lawyer from the city legal department arrived with a document containing my agreement not to sue the department or anyone else. At noon, in time for the early news, the department issued a press release revealing that it had vigilantly and diligently uncovered an unfortunate miscarriage of justice, and, yes, a committee of officers was being created to study methods to prevent future misconduct by informants.

Just after noon, Kit telephoned with more marching orders. I was to be back down at her shop by two o'clock.

The receptionist pointed to a door, and I went in. Kit wasn't there. Carson Talmadge Ritter, Jr, was.

For the first time in a long time, there was warmth in my father's handshake and, wonder of wonders, warmth in his eyes.

'Congratulations, Sonny. Kit told me everything. Let me come right to the point. I think I judged you rather too harshly about your . . . incident. I realize we all make mistakes. I'd like to forget the past and look to the future.'

I was touched and at a loss for words.

'Well, thanks, Dad. Kit's a helluva woman. A helluva lawyer.'

'She is that. You two make a good team. Perhaps sometime we can discuss the possibility of you joining our team.'

'That would be good . . . that would be good. It never hurts to talk.'

What was I supposed to say? That I'd rather work in a soup kitchen than join his team of stuffed partridges dedicated to protecting the corporations and foundations of the world from the great unwashed?

'Your mother would like you to come over

for dinner,' Father said. 'This weekend, eh? Say Saturday at seven. Nothing real formal.'

'Love to. Saturday at seven.'

He cleared his throat. He had bent over to place one step in a bridge, and I knew it wasn't easy for him.

'Well, then,' he said. 'Someone else wants to talk to you. Out there.'

Meg was waiting outside. She wore the black-and-white polka-dot dress I didn't buy her. I saw something new in her eyes. It was an old look I hadn't seen in a long time.

'Hi, Sonny. I want to ask you a direct question and get a direct answer. Do you really call here every morning to listen to my voice?'

'Well, maybe not every morning. I might have missed a few days. Love your message.'

'I'm surprised and . . . well, surprised. I'm sorry we haven't talked as much as we should. Maybe we can have lunch. I'm free right now.'

'I can't think of anything I'd like more,' I said.

For the first time in three years, my ex-wife revealed that sweet smile only I could see.

Kit was standing outside her office, looking disgustingly pleased with herself. I shook my finger at her.

'Under that beautiful lawyer's hide beats

the heart of a sentimentalist,' I said. 'Just answer one question for me, will you? Where the hell did you get the name 'Richard Bleeker'?'

Those lovely blue eyes had the gleam of the poker player who's raking in the biggest pot of the night on a bluff.

'He was my high school algebra teacher,' she said. 'I hated algebra.'

29

No one expected the economy to do a Humpty Dumpty act. What looked like minor slippage proved to be anything but, and, whoops, we had a great fall. The experts who had failed to forecast the recession clogged the TV screens with a variety of revisionist explanations. The voters reacted in the way voters usually do. They blamed the incumbents. Even with strong support from the state Fraternal Order of Police, the governor lost a close race. Of course that meant Larry Lynch was out of a job. If gloating is a sin, I sinned knowingly and joyously.

Unfortunately, and predictably, Larry's unemployment ended all too quickly. He signed on as chief counsel for the county prosecutor's office, a haven for Republican functionaries. In that capacity, Kit told me later, Larry claimed to have pushed the deal for Jeremiah Jackson. Kit didn't believe him, not that it made any difference.

One chalky winter's morning, I sat at the defense table in Judge Jerry Able's Criminal Court and watched Kit end the case. There really wasn't much to do. The agreement had been worked out over a matter of months. The Supreme Court had ordered a new trial, and neither side wanted to risk going to a jury. Hence, a compromise had been designed to fit today's favorite catchword, closure. Judge Able, who was well-named and well-respected, recognized this was the justice system's version of a tire patch.

Wearing a plain brown suit, white shirt buttoned at the top, without tie, and new black shoes, Jackson stood in front of the bench, his long fingers tapping nervously against the side of his slacks. His mother sat in the front row, gripping the Reverend Foster's hand. A dozen spectators watched.

'Have you read the agreement in its entirety, and do you understand the terms of the agreement?' the judge asked.

Jackson spoke in a low voice. 'Yes, sir, and I do.'

'Do you understand that the terms of this agreement are the only terms? In other words, nothing can be implied or construed outside this agreement?'

'Yes, sir.'

'What I'm emphasizing, Mr Jackson, is that the conditions set out herein are the only conditions, no matter what anyone has suggested or implied. Do you understand that?'

'I do, judge.'

'Has anyone told you anything to suggest that if there's any breach of this agreement, you'll be able to assert a claim beyond the terms of the agreement?'

'No, sir.'

Able cleared his throat. 'Very well. You understand that if I accept this agreement, you are pleading guilty to the crime of second-degree murder?'

'Yes, sir.'

'Did you, in fact, commit the crime of second-degree murder, as set out in this agreement?'

Jackson dropped his eyes. 'Yes, sir.'

'Do you understand that if I accept this agreement, you will be under supervision of the state for a period of five years?'

'I do, sir. Five years.'

'And if you violate the conditions of probation in any manner, you will be remanded to the Department of Corrections, to be incarcerated for any and all of the time remaining?'

'Yes, sir.'

The judge lifted his spectacles. 'Make no mistake, Mr Jackson. The court won't tolerate the slightest thing to suggest you're returning to your old ways, to the way of life that put you in this situation in the first place. I won't listen to any song and dance, any sob story. You're at the end of the plank. One wrong step and the sharks can have you. Understand?'

'I do, judge. I don't want to come back.'

'And I don't want to see you again. Very well. Anything further from the state?'

A young deputy prosecutor had the case, and he told Able no.

Kit had nothing further.

'The court accepts the agreement,' Able said. 'The defendant is released, subject to the jurisdiction of the probation department.'

'Hallelujah,' Mrs Jackson said, loud enough for the judge to hear, but he was already disappearing into the door leading to his chambers.

A smiling Kit turned to me with her eyebrows raised, and I smiled back. By the time I looked around, the spectators had left. I grabbed my top-coat and hurried out the door to catch the man who had been sitting by himself in the back row. I thought he might be on the elevator already, but he was waiting in the hallway, a distinguished older gentleman with a white moustache and a tan top-coat folded over his arm.

'Congratulations,' Leland Hurt said. 'I'm sure Mr Jackson will be a model citizen from here on out.' He smiled wryly.

'You're the last person I expected to see here,' I said.

'Well, I didn't come down for any celebration. I came here to tell you that you were right and I was wrong. You were good for me, Mr Ritter. You helped wake me up.'

'I did?'

'If you don't care about the fate of one person, you eventually won't care about the fate of anyone. Compassion is a precious commodity because the world seems to have so little left. You reminded me of that.'

'If you want to thank me, you can buy me a cup of coffee.'

'Not here. I used to work here. Can't say as I care for their coffee. How about the City Market?'

'Fine with me.'

As we waited for the elevator, I said, 'I suppose you read about Tunney and Buckley?'

A federal grand jury had indicted Tunney, Buckley, and three other men on charges of interstate trafficking in stolen property. I knew about the investigation long before it hit the front page of the *Chronicle*, because Venus had called, scared about being approached by the FBI. I arranged for her to get a good lawyer, but it turned out she didn't need one, because she really didn't know anything. Anyway, she was apologetic and thankful, and excited to tell me she planned to get married for the fourth time, and I laughed when she said, 'Well, practice makes perfect, don't it?'

Hurt revealed his wry smile again as he squeezed into the next elevator car. 'I assume you'll be representing Mr Tunney or Mr Buckley and reaping handsome fees.'

'They wisely retained other counsel.'

The elevator slowly reached the main floor, and we crossed through the west wing.

'Still working at the liquor store?' I asked.

'No, I gave that up. Teaching journalism part-time, two days a week. I figured, what the hell, if I can put one young person on the right track, it'd be a small contribution to the public welfare.'

'Good for you, Mr Hurt. Good for you.'

Outside, the wind snapped around the corners of the buildings and bit into our faces. We stood on the corner waiting for the light to change. An old white Cadillac honked as it passed, and I saw Mrs Jackson waving her hand from the passenger seat in the front.

As the car slowly accelerated into the chilly gray morning, I had a glimpse of a face through the back window. I thought I saw the glint of a gold tooth, like the gleam from the eye of a tiger as it returned to the jungle.